T0131679

MENTAL IMMORTALITY

THE CURE FOR MENTAL IMPRISONMENT

PATRICK LEMON

To order additional copies of this book, contact:
Xlibris Corporation
1-888-795-4274
www.Xlibris.com
Orders@Xlibris.com
103171

CONTENTS

1RST PHASE

Develop Immunity from Fear and Intimidation

2ND PHASE

Free Your Mind

3RD PHASE

Develop a Strong Mindset

4TH PHASE

Develop a Strong Heart

5TH PHASE

Develop Mental Awareness (Character Counts)

6TH PHASE

Process of A Mental Rebirth

7TH PHASE

Developing Definite Truth, Ultimate Peace, Happiness, and Power

8TH PHASE

Psychological Preparation: Long-term Thinking

MENTAL IMPRISONMENT

Mental Imprisonment is the opposite of what Mental Immortality offers and grantees, because Mental Imprisonment takes away, conceals, and controls your freedom, controls your ability to gain control, independence, strength, confidence, greatness, happiness,health, power, vision, leadership,peace, creates fear and disguises truth. Mental Imprisonment is when people think they are free, only because they are not locked within a physical cell, jail, or are not forcibly constraint and confined against their will, at least that is what they think. But in reality they do not have free will at all and really are forced against their will, but do not realize it. They do not have free will, because their mentality is controlled and developed by the will of others. Inmates of Mental Imprisonment do not realize that they are locked up, because their eyes trick them into believing they are free, because they have the ability to physically go anywhere they desire to and they can communicate and talk to whomever they please. In actuality they still are only physically allowed to go as far as what their mentality will allow. So optically it looks like they are free, but mentally they are so far from it. They are not free because they cannot think, feel, believe, experience, understand or have conversation on higher levels beyond what imprisons them, controls them and keeps them lost, stuck, traveling in circles, miserable, without hope, without purpose and trapped within a limited and controlled destiny. Those stuck within Mental Imprisonment are inmates and are the warden too, but don't know they are the warden too. They only become the warden once they realize they are in Mental Imprisonment, which that realization allows them the choice and power to become the warden and use the key to unlock themselves out and become free.

MENTAL IMMORTALITY

Mental Immortality guarantees the total and definite release of a inmate and grantees a new start, a new life, a new destiny, and a whole different way of feeling and being. Mental Immortality changes the future history of past and future generations to come! Which within my book I constructed eight phases of disconnecting from Mental Imprisonment. Which with each disconnection you will be entering higher levels toward Mental Immortality until at the end of the eighth phase you will have gained Mental Immortality. These phases will create and cause separation from Mental Imprisonment and deception, which thee affect will open up portals from within: portals of power, portals of true truth, independence, portals of strength, portals of greatness, portals of higher awareness, portals of long lasting survival, portals of fearlessness, portals of health, portals of happiness and peace, portals of vision and leadership. Which these portals will liberate you towards Mental Immortality. As you continue to read through each phase you are gaining: higher understanding, deeper strength, bravery, you are healing, you are coming alive, you are becoming what you never knew you could, you are rerouted towards perfection, you are gaining freedom knowledge, until at the end you will receive what was taken away from you from the beginning of time, which is the secret gift and power of true freedom by which I offer through the process of Mental Immortality!

My book is a manuscript that offers the following: positive psychology, reflective psychology, self-improvement psychology, self-knowledge psychology, therapy, spirituality, sociology, philosophy, workology, streetology, survivology (higher survival awareness /

teens and adults), and is a parental guide. This is a book that answers questions that you yourself maybe didn't know you needed to ask. Or answers questions you yourself didn't know you needed answers too. In addition my book was written and its purpose is to show others that you have the power to create much more opportunities and choices based upon redefining yourself and refocusing your focus beyond your given or forced perspectives. Now you will have the power of knowing what to focus on and give your time too, which will allow you to be the person you need to be and will give you more control over yourself and your experiences. Which will ultimately produce a healthy and self-empowering productive way of thinking. This book is also is a guide and path developer for children that do not have anyone to turn to for conscious advice and guidance, whether boys or girls. Which this wisdom will show them how to take control of themselves and their life before they and their life stir out of control. Within my book I take you toward a natural high mental state of mind in conjunction to higher levels of emotional states of bliss. The purpose of my book is to raise consciousness, encourage, empower, strengthen, mentally elevate, and inspire people toward happiness, peace, power, financial riches, and to gain higher survival instinct awareness. My book is power knowledge and destiny changing information! This is a novel to point people in the direction of success and to redirect a destiny and fate of misery, unhappiness, and financial failure toward a destiny of happiness, peace, freedom, deep strength, fearlessness, financial prosperity, courage, inspiration, extra-ordinariness, and greatness beyond measure!

INTRODUCTION: MY STORY

Once upon a time I restricted my abilities, capabilities, and endless possibilities. That is, until I found a way to unlock my hidden strengths, gifts, and secrets. These gifts and secrets were only hidden, because I never searched for them. But, I never knew they were there until I payed attention to my own attention, then forced my attention into the direction of everything that made me stronger and wiser as opposed to allowing my attention to be controlled by everything that was ignorant and misleading. "There is always a way out of something if there was a way in, and the way out has always been inside you,"(Lemon). You have to find out a way to get inside yourself. The way to get inside of you is to give yourself your full undivided attention. You will always be lost, without the right direction, and confused if you never invest your attention toward yourself. Remember that it all starts with you and guess what it all ends with you too. So with that saying in order to control or even better recreate your start and end you must invest your attention toward you. You must find a way to find yourself before it is to late and the results will be everybody has found a way inside you but you. So now you have all these people who are in you and never left and now you dont even have room for you to be in you. You will be powerless, because initially you were lost already, which validates you never finding yourself and now you are so far from your true potential, strength, right path, and gifts. Which you will live a life of being manipulated and totally controlled and guided into the direction that everybody else wants you to go even if you do not desire too. The way to get inside you is to stop paying attention to everything that is external and everything that is on the outside. The way that you receive strength beyond measure is refocusing your attention inwardly, because everything in the inside will make you stronger. You do not get real strength and reach your highest potential by focusing on outside things or external things that control your attention.

Initially my focus and perspectives would not allow me to search and find my true potential and gifts. It was at this point of a new found perspective, which gave me the power to refocus on everything that made me stronger! That new perspective opened up my perception and showed me how to focus on unlocking me! "You cannot focus on anything that is not within the boundaries of what you know," (Lemon). Sometimes you must think outside of what you know in order to make sure what you know is what you need to know and is beneficial for you to know and not knowledge that will keep you limited or restricted. So as I searched beyond the clouds of hope I finally found the what I needed and was looking for. If you do not search, you will never study, and if you never study you will never gain knowledge to master anything. I took control of my perspectives, which gave me control and power over my life and destiny. I finally found that everything that you seek and look for in this world is closer than you think. If your focus is below how God wants us all to feel, which is happy, peaceful, fulfilled, and successful then you can never reach higher more powerful levels of feelings of inspiration, confidence, and discipline. Anything you search for, whether it is finding purpose or truth, it all is inside you. You just have to make time to focus on a unique way to unlock it and use it. Sometimes I think that people do not even know themselves as well as they believe that they do. How could you if you never focused your focus on yourself or you never spent any time directed toward yourself in order to show you how you need to think and be.

After I found my gift, the eyes within my mind were open and I became something worth becoming! I became greatness! "I believe nothing is a gift until you open it. The only way to turn a gift into a present is to stop living in the past," (Lemon). I believe that no one is born with a gift or talent; everything must be developed through practice, patience, diligence, faith, dedication, concentration, focus, time, and most importantly through discipline and patience. I had to break out of what was concealing my true potential. Although it has been said that curiosity killed the cat! "In my case, I know that curiosity healed the cat," (Lemon)! I received a message, obtained, and retained the message. I listened to it and changed for the better towards happiness, peace, greatness, and financial success. Although I'd heard the message, it was ultimately my decision to apply what I'd learned and devise a plan of action towards change. So that is what changed me; my deciding and making the choice to change.

There was something I felt like I was missing in my life. I just felt a bit lost, unwise, unhappy, and overwhelmingly negative. I realized that I was thinking in the wrong way and I was thinking in a way that was not beneficial to me or others. I was fed up with not being as extraordinary and exceptional as I was capable of being. I felt as though there had to be a way to alter this potentially life threatening destiny and fate of discontent and financial poverty. I realized that the only thing that was in deficiency was my lack of mental awareness of my own mental abilities; So it was only safe to say that, physically, this is how I lived my life, based upon how I thought.

WHAT A COINCIDENCE?

I believe ultimately when things happen one after the other in an order and sequential pattern after a while these are not coincidences. My strong belief and opinion is when events in your life generate coincidence after coincidence, it becomes apparent that it is a pattern, and closely in sequential order it becomes too close to reality a destiny, a fate, and how your life was meant to be, who you was meant to become, and where you was destined to go. However this is only meant to be based upon if you think in the same way of this pattern, order, and coincidence.

[MENTAL IMPRISONMENT]

Mental Imprisonment is a jail within a jail. It is a war within a war. It is always a much deeper war than the one that is presented to you physically. A war is always powered by and its main weapon is the art of deception. In order to start a physical war, it must internalize in the mind first. Mental imprisonment is a war of complete control over you in regards to the following: with holding the truth, your mind, spirit, soul, creativity, life, happiness, peace, power, survival, focus, perspective, perception, financial life style, time, experiences, attitude, how you feel, energy, and destiny. Your body is the prison and your mind is the cell. It ultimately sets up your destiny and fate toward a path of failure, financial deterioration and poverty, discouragement, inhibited and limited experiences, high levels of doubt, fear, unhappiness, misery, self-defeat, negativity, limited perspectives, mental and emotional trauma. This path was created by a circle of historical patterns that stem from limited knowledge and distorted negative restricted perspectives that forms your perception, which ultimately creates your beliefs and reality as you understand and know it. Which if these perspectives are not transformed and reconstructed; they become a hereditary and passed down generational negative out of control self-destructive effect. "A perception that inhibits any level of growth and consciousness is slavery within a world where you think you are free," (Lemon). This prison to a certain high extent can do the following if you allow yourself to serve a life sentence : lay and plan your life out and how you possibly will be, from where you will go, how far you will go, how unsuccessful you will be, how unhappy you will be, how lost you will be, how least knowledge you will have, to the negative experiences you will have, to the unbenificial and type of people you will come in contact with, to all the dangerous and life threatening situations you will be in, to the conversations that will not be productive or useful for you to have, to the low status level you will be a part of, to the environment you will live in, to how little will be possible for you, to what will not be available to you, to how unhealthy you will be, to how negative you will be, to how many options you will have, to what you focus on, to all the useless activities you use your mind for and spend your time on, to all the limited choices you will have, to all the limited opportunities you will be presented, to ultimately as I said before to what your overall perception and reality will be. "No one could have never had any control over something that is above what their reality will not allow them to focus on or gave time too," (Lemon). It is as if you become so far behind yourself that you do not even know anything about who you are. Mental imprisonment puts you so far behind yourself it will cause you to be completely out of touch with yourself and ultimately presents you with a life that is completely lost and out of control! Nobody can know who they are if they never had any control over the person they became.

I compare mental imprisonment to physically being incarcerated, but a lot worse, because physically at least when you are behind bars and stuck within the inside you have no concrete self knowledge as to what's really happening on the outside but by hearsay. However, it is a lot worse when you are mentally behind bars, because you will never know what's on the other side of your mind, because your mind is restricting your mind from seeing the beauty, happiness, and fortune that everyone has the ability to acquire. "You cannot see beauty if your mind is not beautiful," (Lemon).

The worst thing about it is you do not know what beauty and freedom is inside of your mind, because you are too busy looking at everybody else and focusing on all the physical aspects of the world. It is where you think you are free only because you can physically go and roam where ever you want to go.

However, "how can you really be free if you cannot see past the same perception that imprisoned you and forced you to focus on everything that took time away from you gaining consciousness and power,"(Lemon)? If it was up to me I would diagnose this as a mental disorder that stops ones ultimate mental abilities and stripes people from greatness and happiness. It is the worst war that can be waged against you, because it is a war to keep you confined within yourself. But to break free from this prison you must first know you are the key to your own jail cell. You will always be imprisoned and defeated until you gain (WOMSC) weapons of mass self-consciousness. Once you gain new perspective of yourself, and what you're true inner power is, and the world, then you will have time to prepare to make yourself great! "Once you become your own archeologist and research developer you will find missing pieces of the history of your-self. Which that history will reveal the secret that was always suppose to be the mystery of your misery," (Lemon).

[MENTAL IMMORTALITY]

(Disconnection)
The Cure

Mental immortality is the cure for mental imprisonment! Mental immortality is what you receive once a disconnection from mental imprisonment happens. This disconnection provides the following: more control over your life, spirit, soul, higher healthier perceptions, power, freedom, happiness, peace, provides higher survival awareness, higher consciousness alters destiny and opens up new realms of opportunities, choices, and experiences. Mental Immortality gives you higher understanding about yourself and guides you to find a better you. Also Mental Immortality makes the unthinkable thinkable, the impractical practical, the unrealistic realistic, the unimaginable imaginable and the impossible possible! "It is said that Christopher Columbus discovered America, but the greatest discovery one can discover is thee existence of themselves," (Lemon). The cure for mental imprisonment is discovering yourself and how you came into existence, then reconstructing your born into existence and transforming your existence beyond what you ever thought was possible. This is how you recreate and rebuild your destiny, happiness, peace, and your power.

Mental Immortality gives you ultimate confidence, but prevents arrogance. I don't believe in being arrogant, because from my understanding arrogance destines one to fall from grace. Arrogance can destine one to ultimately lose or get killed, because one becomes too cocky and begins to defy and underestimate the challenger, enemy, but most important the creator God. Arrogance puts one in the league of vulnerability, because people become too busy gloating and mentally stays on a high horse to high to realize that it is a weakness. Ultimately, they get distracted and forget the original mission, plan, and purpose sometime. For example, I was watching this basketball movie and within the movie there was 20 seconds left on the clock and it was the 4ᵗʰ quarter, the score was 76(bulldogs) to 77(Lions) and the Bull Dogs had possession, so the best player on the Bull Dogs came down and made a 3 pointer making it 79 to 77 Bull Dogs with 12 seconds left. Now the Lions quickly passed the ball in and in the mean time the best player who scored the shot for the Bull Dogs was soaking in his own arrogance and shine by being caught in the moment of his fame and physically replaying a example of his shot and forgot to get back on defense, because the game was not over yet apparently. However, the other team rapidly ran down the floor and hit a two pointer and scored the final winning shot and made the score 80 Lions to 79 Dogs. That was just an example of arrogance leads to defeat, because of lack of humility. Also, Mental Immortality gives you ultimate determination and motivation that one needs for success in this world and you will realize that nobody can stop you. Dream of how far you will physically go and how much happier experiences you will have. You must mentally take yourself their so when you physically get there; it will be an easier transformation. You will go places and conquer all you set out to do with no one in your path of success and happiness.

You have to make a way out of no way. But the only reason there is no way, because you haven't thought of a different solution that brings positive results. It is a way of freeing your mind, enhancing, elevating, and expanding it in a positive innovative way. I believe God the creator made us in the spirit of his own image and his image is the image of a powerful, positive, righteous, humble, honest, and just God. But, like a father and a son's relationship in the way a son should sustain the utmost respect for the one that made him, we must do the same as well by honoring and respecting the one who created us all.

Mental Immortality will allow you to soar higher than an eagle and into the clouds of light, financial success, happiness and pure bliss. However, you must maintain and sustain humility. The definition of humility is being marked by meekness or modesty in behavior, attitude and spirit; not arrogant or prideful. You must maintain a good humble mind and heart and still overall be an open minded person that is a likeable person. For instance, if you developmental immortality, you will be able to achieve anything and everything, when others will wonder how on earth do you do what you do?! When you gain this gift, you will have already accepted the fact no one can bring you down but you. Because now you are too high and elevated to even hear the voices of doubters and negative thinkers. This will bring you out of your doubtful, limiting, and negative state of mind. Ultimately giving you mental independence, freedom, and will give you the gift of what I call Mental Immortality.

The disconnection from Mental Imprisonment, The Journey toward Mental Immortality, freedom, power, happiness, survival, a new Life and destiny begins Now!

8 Phases to Cure Mental Imprisonment: The Journey Toward Mental Immortality

1RST PHASE

(Develop Immunity from Fear
and Intimidation)

Once you are intimidated, fear someone, a group of people or something, this means that you are controlled by what ever it is that you fear. This is a detrimental trait of mental imprisonment. Also this is one of the highest levels of mental imprisonment. Everyone has had something they fear or feared, so don't ever believe anything different. Whether its a fear of success, failure, love, and many more, so everybody please do not act as if you do not know what I am talking about, (laughing). Some people have a fear of snakes, spiders, stinky breathe, onion crying chitterlings feet and its a shame when even the inside of your ear smells like morning breathe and expired milk(laughing) this is everybody cue to laugh if you didn't!!! To not fear something means to know and understand it. Ultimately knowing and understanding how it works will give you the same power it has, which will give you the same weapons it has that it uses against you. In addition now you can use the same weapons it has plus your own to fight it and defeat it. To know and understand something is to focus on it. People do not focus on anything that they do not want to become. In considering what I just said, I think people fall victim to the things they do not focus on. A lot of times the opposite of what you don't want to focus on and become is what makes you fear it. Some fall victim to what they don't focus on or what they don't want to become, because they do not understand it.

[POWER]

"Innocence is neiveness and weakness in a world founded upon and ran by the guilty," (Lemon). If you are a good person and focuses on being good, sometime good people fall victim to bad intentioned people, because they are naive to what evil people focus on. I am not saying focus on what you do not want to become, but understand that there are people who focus on the opposite that you do, which their focus is not positive or good. Be aware, understand, and know when you are around those who do not focus on what you focus on. You will know and you will feel it, because their energy and spirit is not like yours is. Being a good person isn't enough to survive among bad intentioned people. You can still stay a good person in a world of evil. But you must not be foolish and ignorant toward the motives of those that see goodness as weakness or a opportunity to plot against you. You just have to be strong and gain knowledge of both sides, so you will know when and how to defend yourself. You'll be much healthier and stronger deciding to be a good person. If you decide to be a good person, then you are a leader and you will get an abundance of happiness and riches without the burden of enemies hunting you for the evil you have done to them if you choose to do wrong by everyone. A Good person is a powerful person, because they are not afraid to be different, be happy, and be themselves. People who make a choice to be a negative and a wrong intentioned person are much more mentally and physically sicker, they are less happy, have no peace, they are always in unlucky situations, they are lonely, they are followers of conformity, and they are insecure.

[THE SUPER HERO AND THE VILLAIN]

I compare power in this context between two focuses of a super hero and a villain. For example, in this movie I saw there were a super hero and a villain. The super hero initially didn't know he had super human powers, but he knew something was different about him, he just didn't know what. However, one day he ran into the villain who knew he was a villain and had already accepted his role in the world as a villain. The villain told the super hero that one day we will see each other again. The super hero looked at the villain with confusion. Ultimately the villains prophecy came true and they ran into each other again, but this time for a fight, which by this time the super hero finally found who he was and embraced his powers. The villain told the super hero I told you that we would meet again. The villain told him you are just like me, basically trying to manipulate the super hero for purposes to become partners and become unstoppable together to completely take over the world. But the super hero told him that I am nothing like you, but actually he was in some ways like him, but just choose to embrace and only practice the better side of his power for purposes of good instead of feeding the other powerful side of him, which would create destruction. My point is they both were extremely powerful forces and had the same powers to a certain extent. However, the huge difference which separated the two was each had different focuses and practices. The super hero used his power to focus on good, but the villain used his power to focus on evil. Whatever is powerful it either will be used as good or it will be used as evil. Knowledge is Power and whoever has it you will know how they are using it based upon what their focus is most of the time. "Knowledge is power, but knowledge becomes magic once practiced," (Lemon).

THE POWER OF WHY?

It seems as though everyone interrogates everybody else but themselves. I guess this would create a scared straight mirror reflection of the truth about yourself. "You cannot be true to yourself if you do not know why you cannot see the truth in yourself," (Lemon). The power, solution, answer, and healing is within the WHY questions. It will not be to long before you find the answer to WHY questions. However, the challenge comes when asking and forming the WHY questions. Asking that question and putting that question in the proper order is the challenging part. The why reveals the complete understanding, the big picture of all problems and will redirect your life, health, and destiny. The why will open up unto you true knowledge without limitation and will get you to think critically. Which will allow you to understand how you actually got to your answer and solution? The why gives you the power of prophecy, because it will reveal to you future consequences before the fact or before something will occur. Basically knowing why helps you to stop future mistakes and negative situations that possibly will arise. The why creates vision within you which will project outward and will turn you into a great leader! So in reality now you will know what is coming your way and now you have the power of choice not to go that route. The answers are just a means to validate the curiosity of the questions, which are important too, but not as crucial as developing higher level why questions. Always find the why and you will always find more knowledge, power, control, which will open more doors and routes for happiness, peace, freedom, and opportunities. You cannot make an application of any knowledge beyond what you were not taught or beyond the why questions that you have not asked. For example, within one of the movies the Matrix, one of the most dangerous and ruthless villain said to NEO, "the thing that makes us powerful and separates us from them is we know WHY," Basically them knowing why this happens and why that happens places them on another level of power. Finding why is power! Finding the why will give you the knowledge to practice it. For example, say someone has a problem and they do not know why they have this issue, but you know why they have the problem they do. Who has more power you or the person who does not know why they have that problem? The answer is you have more power then the person with the problem, because if you know why something is the way it is, then you have the power to find a solution, answer, truth, and the power to heal. Finding the why will change your perspective and give you the truth. Finding the why will break you free from anything negative that is suppressing and controlling you. Finding the why will give you knowledge above the problem or situation. In order to find the why and the truth you must ask and seek the right questions.

"No one can ask any questions or gain any answers to anything that is above and beyond the level of knowledge that they posses," (Lemon). Just by this statement alone puts you so far from the truth, from what you need to know, who you need to be, so far from an answer, and a solution. In addition you cannot find any answers or solutions without developing higher knowledge which will create higher level questions which will lead to the truth and power. You cannot control a problem, find a solution, or change anything that you do not know that it is a problem. How could you know if you have problems if you do not have the level of self-knowledge that would reveal to you that you have this problem? You cannot get to the bottom of the why if you do not even realize you have problems. You must start asking the right questions first in order to gain powerful answers that would change your life completely. The first thing you must do in order to find the answer to the most important question (which is why) is you must be honest. You cannot find a solution to any problem without first being honest about any situation. The way you find the powerful why questions is through going deep. You cannot get to the bottom of anything without going deep within it. "If you are not willing to go deep in the depths of darkness, then you will always be on the surface thinking you're in the light, but within the lies you will find real light and truth and that truth of light lies within the darkness,"(Lemon).

For example, if a man or woman jumps off of a mountain top. Everyone will ask who? What mountain top? Where was him or her? How could she or he do this? However in order to get to the bottom of this situation, the big question that will reveal all truth and clear all assumptions will be why did he or she jump off the mountain top? The why is what separates you from not being in control of your happiness, success, peace, and destiny. The why is what separates you from better and healthier experiences. The why is what separates and comes between you and power.

"Not knowing the why is what segregates you from how you need to think now and who you need to be in the future," (Lemon). Without knowing why you are you and how you became you, you will never have any power. Why is what separates you from love. How can you love anybody else if you do not know why you cannot love yourself? "Become a spy and submerge within to gather top secret information on yourself to find the why," (Lemon). Find and search for the why, within yourself then you will find the truth within yourself. This truth of you will give you power. Once you find the why you will find you. If you search for the why eventually you will find the answer. The answer to the why will be your solution will give you complete power and control over the situation, which you are the situation. "You are an out of control situation until you search for and find the solution to the why," (Lemon). The why is you! The secret is within. All power is inside.

THE GAME

(Control)

Lack of knowledge produces fear. Also the lack of not knowing why or what is the cause of your fear produces fear. Both the lack of knowledge and fear will inevitably subject you to a reality of totally being controlled, miserable, and living a life of fear and powerlessness. This is why some are subjected to being totally controlled, because of their lack of knowledge and not knowing why. If you do not know why you need to know why, then you will be so far from knowledge and freedom, but will completely emerge in the depths of control. When I talk about control in this context I mean control in aspects of people whose main objectives are to keep others so far in the dark, so far from deeper knowledge, so far from the truth that they only have the option to live in fear. Confidence is great, but only can go so far. Confidence will break you from fear, but knowledge will strip you from control and bring you to the light from those who want you in the dark. Knowledge and confidence together will free you from both fear and control. No one can control or put fear into a confident person with knowledge. This person is too independent, knowledgeable, and powerful. I think one reason a person is controlled and posses fear, because of their extreme levels of co-dependence and very limited and minimal knowledge. Gain independence through being confident and gain control through gaining more knowledge. "A person with confidence is a force, but a person with confidence and knowledge knows why," (Lemon).

THE GAME

Part 2
(Hate/ Control)

"Hate and control does not mix, unless someone knows a secret that makes them feel inadequate," (Lemon). Why would someone still make a choice to decide to hate someone that they supposedly control? The reason is, because they know knowledge about this person they control that produces fear and hate inside them that becomes the motive and reason why to focus on keeping a person controlled and unknowledgeable. Furthermore, some hate others they control is because they know a truth that doesn't set them free, but actually it makes them feel powerless. So, a person could generate hate, then turn that hate into wanting to control, by making sure they without hold this truth and knowledge from a person.

It doesn't make sense to hate someone that you control, because you already have everything that they need, want, and hope for. If someone has everything anyone could possibly want and desire, for that person to posses hate for those they have exceedingly more than, means they in reality they know the one thing that they never had and never will have is what those control retain and is what makes them hate and become jealous. In addition that one thing money cannot buy and it is a historical knowledge and truth that no one cannot change. But the one thing that they can do is with hold this powerful knowledge and truth. Which with holding this knowledgeable truth will inevitably control and limit those who are subjected to this evil. Ultimately that knowledge that makes them fear those they think they control forces them to try to stripe any peace and happiness from those they control. But really this is a false and untrue illusion of a sense of control and power, because anyone who needs any control over anyone in order to feel good is a weak and powerless person. Also they posses more fear then the person or people they are trying to control, so obviously they are being controlled by their own fear of the ones that they think they control. Also the ones who set out to control people and make others life miserable are in actuality the ones who are the most miserable and the sickest. The most powerful people are the ones who focus on the pursuit of their own happiness and the happiness of others. These people will always have the most control over their lives and will help others gain the same control over their lives.

"Knowledge is power for others, but knowledge is fear for the ones who control and limit others potential," (Lemon). The knowledge that the person knows about the one they control is what actually creates fear and hate in them, because this knowledge proves that the ones they think they control is actually more powerful and stronger than they are. Which they make sure they control this person by never revealing the knowledge of who they really are, what they are truly capable of, and how powerful they really are. "Hating is a disease, but I wish them all the best and I hope they get well soon," (Lemon). The most powerful is the controlled. However, the main reason they are controlled is that they do not know that they posses such power. Those who know they have such power are the ones who make sure the controlled do not know this. If the controlled knew this, then this would give them too much, knowledge, power, and control over themselves. If you do not know your history you will never understand your true power, which will always be the reason why you are controlled.

[FEAR]

In A different Light

Fear is an illusion of whats not real, it is made up, and is a creation of what master manipulators of the human psyche has made an art form of control and to prohibit any independence or freedom. But sole purpose is to develop a life time of dependance. Fear is only as real as what you believe it to be. Historically fear is the oldest and deepest internal connection that we all share. In addition fear was never a negative or a bad thing. Fear originally is positive and is a good thing, until this knowledge got into the wrong hands. Fear is a natural response that helps us know when there is danger lurking and it is our natural defense mechanism as human beings. Fear is just a response that originates and triggers our nervous system to respond accordingly to what we perceive as a threat or danger. As I said prior fear was accepted as a good thing that is until people who knew this knowledge made the choice to test and experiment controlling the majority through massively triggering fear responses that stir our nervous systems completely out of control. These fear responses are triggered and controlled through making sure that our focus is always on everything that creates us to live in a reality of fear. The ones who control and deliberately force a fear based recipe within our home cooked meals. They make sure they control our focus to focus on everything that creates fear which comes in forms of the following:television, depictions, visuals, stereotypes, forced perspectives, and audios through media presentations that describe the latest weather disasters, the latest violent acts, a prophecy of when the world ends, war predictions, economic and financial scares, terrorists retaliation, etc. In addition technology is great, but however can make it a lot easier and can give people who use the bad form of fear more leverage through raising the fear alert. In addition they can put fear into people a lot faster than usual. Also technology gives these people a wider window through avenues of internet, cell phones, etc. These fears create an attitude shift which controls your energy and will produce fearful energy. "Fear controls your energy, but knowledge and confidence defeats your enemy," (Lemon). Look at your fears from the perspective of at least your fears gives you something to live for. Look at your fears as a new journey and opportunity that arises and be thankful you have a new job, which will challenge you to bring out your highest potential. As I said prior at least your fears gives you something to live for as opposed to giving up and you living to die.

[BREAK YOUR GOOD RELATIONSHIP WITH FEAR]

"You cannot fear anything that you do not allow to exist and the thing that connects you to its existence is communication," (Lemon). Fears foundation of development and growth is created by all physical and external based stimulus or outside views. Fear is not initially internal. You were not born with fear! Fear is not natural. Anything natural is from GOD and this is how you know fear is not real, because all that is real is from GOD and gives you strength, power, and health, because all that is real is natural and is from GOD. Fear is not real until you allow the physical, external, and material world control you. If you do not communicate with fear then it cannot hunt you or control you. In reality in order to defeat your fears you must stop communicating so much with the physical and external. In another translation you must stop allowing your focus to be controlled by everything external. The more you allow yourself to be controlled by physical and material things then the less power you will have, which the effect will create more fear and misery. The more you communicate and allow physical things to control you then the more fear you will have. You must connect to something from the inside in order to be fearless. In order to destroy fear you must be powerful from within. You cannot destroy fear when all you can see is what fear shows you. You can not be fearless by trusting anything physical or outside of you to free you. You must have vision past fear in order to destroy it and any vision past fear is not from the perspective of anything physical, it will always be internal. If you do not build a strong inside then everything on the outside will control you, make you powerless, and cause a life of fear. Also if you do not find a way to look at things from the inside out as opposed to the outside in, then you will only be living a life of confusion, ignorance, fear, and will be trapped and a slave to what is not even real. What is real and most powerful is always what you do not see. Once you understand this, then you will see fear is not all that its cracked up to be.

Communication is extremely powerful and is our way of connecting to everything, even fear. You cannot be infected, affected, governed by, or controlled by anything that you do not think exist. The only thing that allows it to exist is your level of communication with it. I am not saying ignore your fears, but once you have conquered them or realized that they were not the premises of any facts or anything real, then you have no reason to keep reliving and refocusing on a false fear. So after you have defeated it, why keep reliving what you defeated and got over. Nothing can exist or manifest if you do not communicate with it. What I mean in my view of communication is your focus, paying attention to it either verbally internally or externally connecting to it, which all brings it alive to manifest within you. By communicating with it means you are acknowledging its existence. Also means you are giving it power to manifest and enter your life. Why is it that people have a better relationship with fear as opposed to confidence? Some tend to have a more extraordinary commitment with fear as opposed to power and greatness. To break that commitment you must eliminate your commitment and special bond with it. You must segregate your fear from within, and then integrate confidence in order to escape misery, defeat, and unhappiness. Break your communication with fear, and then you will destroy its existence. Terminate your communication with fear, and then you eradicate your great relationship with it as well. This is what you want, which is a bad and anti-social relationship with it.

You must become anti-social with your fears in order to erase its existence and power. Eradicate all forms of communicating with your fears. In many cases your fears are just illusionary and falsified truths that in reality are misunderstood grounds for nothing real. To understand the premises of your falsified fears you must look behind it and at the beginning of them. Once you do this you will gain connections of understanding the causes of your so-called fears, then you will realize what started them. Ultimately you will see that what you thought you feared really wasn't what you feared at all. You will realize the root of your fears is not anything that actually had grounds to create a real fear and you just thought it was your fears because you were distracted by a false illusion of a very persuasive misinterpreted fear that was created by something physical. What kept your fears alive was the great relationship that you preserved with them through means of communication and allowing them to poison your life. Make a commitment to communicate with everything that brings you power and anything that will bring you power rather then fear will always be something that you can not see, it will always be internal and from within. "True power will always be created by what you do not see, so paying attention to everything physical will always give you a false visual,"(Lemon). What you really need to see is always beyond what you physically see.

[SCARE YOURSELF THE RIGHT WAY]

Scare yourself into being fearless, rather then allowing yourself to posses fear. It seems as though people scare themselves all the wrong ways and even allow others the power and option to put fear into them. Wouldn't it be great if you could have the ability to turn the tables? Well you do have this power and I will show you how to obtain it. Scare yourself into happiness, strength, health, and peace. I believe that we have all the wrong fears. We tend to fear never becoming wealthy, never getting a degree, never achieving high status and position. We have fears of never finding love. We put negative fear into ourselves daily. How about putting positive fear(I call it strength fear too) within you or create positive scare tactics. You should have a fear of never being strong, brave, fearless, happy, courageous, healthy, and confident. You should have a fear of never being great! You should have a fear of never leaving a powerful legacy. Use fear as power and a way to show you that you need to change not allowing fear to stop you from changing. Fear is good when viewed from a positive perspective. You shouldn't have a fear of not being able to make it home from work in time to watch dancing with the stars or old reruns of Seinfeld while laying on the sofa with one sock on eating old steak dinners that you left in the refrigerator three days ago and hoping that it is still eatable,(laughing). Whatever you fear the most will control you whether you know it or not. So wouldn't it be nice to allow your own confidence to be in control of your life and you? Wouldn't it be great to allow your strength to be in control of your life? You should have a fear of never gaining happiness and peace. Which that positive fear will give way to a window of opportunity to open up with in your life for you to change toward accomplishing what you fear. You should scare yourself the right way by scaring yourself into happiness, strength, love, and peace. When you scare yourself in a positive way, this means that you are using fear to your advantage by scaring yourself in order to realize the short-term and long-term effects of these fears. It helps you understand ahead of time the spiritual, mental/psychological, emotional negative risks you are taking by not turning your fears around toward controlling your fears to help you and not harm you. This means you are using fear to create and make sure you stay on the right path toward confidence, bravery, strength, peace, and happiness. "Scare yourself into being fearless,"(Lemon).

INTIMIDATION

Part 1
(Mental Inhibitor)

I label this fear and intimidation as a mental disease and inhibitor. This disease ultimately will not allow you to mentally mature and will stop you from having psychological independence. It confines your confidence. It will stop your mental growth and mind levitation, which will deem you to stay on the same level and you will never be destined for greatness. It will negatively permanently paralyze your potential for greatness. Living life like this will disable any higher feelings of motivation and determination. Fears partner is control, doubt, lies, and high levels of co-dependence. The partner of confidence is freedom, truth, sureness, and high levels of independence. You cannot maintain a perception of fear and think you will find the truth. The truth shall set you free! This is true, truth is knowledge and power. To seek the truth means you are facing your fears. Some people biggest fear is themselves. Some would rather not search themselves for the truth, because they might find too many problems and issues that they don't want to be honest about. Until you are honest with yourself about your fears then you will forever be trapped in a perception of fear. Fear is just an illusion. Fear is not real, it only becomes real when you think about negative situations within your past or you wonder and worry negatively about your future. However, if you are not reliving negative events in your past or negatively wondering about your future in that split moment when you are not doing either, you are fearless! It only becomes real when you react to situations that controls your focus and time. To break free from fear and intimidation you must acknowledge as a problem, and then the solution is to run towards your fears, defeat them, then leave them as a mark on your history. Then you will be thankful for your fears, because without them you wouldn't have anything to conquer, give you motivation, determination, and drive. You become strong when you become thankful for your fears, because without them you would not have ever known how strong you really were. You must look at everything from a positive angle, even through negativity. "Never believe anything, give into, or accept a perception that limits your confidence, peace, and happiness," (Lemon).

Fear and intimidation stunts thinking for yourself and you will be more of a lost follower then a found leader. If you think about it, following sometime can be a dangerous avenue to a quick death. I say this because, most people follow without even putting into perspective what they are actually following. There is nothing wrong with analyzing a plan for you that you yourself have not drew up the blue print for or haven't even seen. It's critical that you develop your own blue print and then compare yours to the person who made one up for you. I bet you will find every time they left out some type of knowledge that would lead you closer to victory and success as opposed to how they constructed their blue print. Consequently, if one doesn't gain such self sufficiency they will always depend on others to think for them and the result is they will always be labeled a follower and never a leader. Also in my opinion the destiny of most followers' future is pre-determined, very simple and limited. Which I am not promoting a campaign to defy leadership, because we have great leaders. I'm simply supporting a mindset of knowing and realizing what you are actually following, so you can be a more knowledgeable and effective follower of something good and something worth following. We have leaders and followers in our world, but the leaders are in a position to lead as well teach and prepare followers to sooner than later become leaders. Leaders must eventually past the torch so it will continue to stay lit!

Preserving fear and intimidation will be the result of never developing a strong heart and will power. A strong heart is the engine for the endurance of a strong mind. Ultimately, if you don't develop both, you will never become a leader. Being intimidated by a person or people will never allow you to think on their level or beyond it. Ultimately your world will be controlled by those who projected thoughts and ideas within your mind that unfortunately created your beliefs, fears, your values, and your purpose of existence. But the most crucial variable is this mind development will become your limited reality of life, the world, and present you with a life of fear. This state of mind of having fear and being intimidated causes you to be extremely vulnerable, unsuccessful and a failure at most or all you do. You must get tired of your fears in order to defeat them.

[NEGATIVE IDOLIZATION]

Part 2

Negative idolization is another form of fear and intimidation. It is very important that you never put people on pedestals. The definition of putting people on pedestals is putting someone in a position of high regard, adoration and idolizing. It is nothing wrong with catering to people or treating them as royalty and making them feel special by recognition. However, it becomes a problem when you yourself don't see yourself as special, royalty, and do not recognize yourself.

Ultimately negatively idolizing people unfortunately sometimes will submit you to become intimidated by them, which gives them a dictator role over your life, decisions, choices, purpose, and destiny. You must dissociate respect from worshiping when it comes to people. It is a thin line between respect and worship. It is only a thin line between respect and worship when referring to someone who does not understand the difference. Do not be tricked into worshiping someone. For example, an unrighteous leader displays this power among young kids who want to be like him/her, wants to be loved, acknowledged, praised, or respected. But, "there is no respect or honor in being a pawn to be used and not for purposes to defeat the king, but just to crush your dreams," (Lemon). Honestly you are just a vessel in other words you are not important, you lack vital information and you are just the protection for the so called protector. Which they don't even see you as protection, they view you as a way to protect the ones who is really the protectors. So you in a way are just a very low level protection for higher level protection that is protecting the protected. So, think about it you will be the first to die, get caught, or go to jail.

So ask yourself is the so called protectors cause worth dying for (make sure you know the true cause) and if so will your death and legacy be acknowledged as honorable or will it be overlooked and thrown into the archives as shameless, pitiful, basic, practical, usual, suspected and swept under the rug as stereotypical. This unrighteous person might tell this kid to go rob or kill someone. This act can sometime go the wrong way and the kid can end up dead, seriously hurt or even caught by the police and end up going to prison doing 20 to life. This person premeditately sent this kid into harms and deaths way, because this unrighteous leader beforehand knew of the dangers. People tend to do things they normally wouldn't for those they are intimidated by and those they put in high regard as compared to putting them on a pedestal and idolization. People use this as a sense of leverage.

Ultimately, I believe after putting people on pedestals your brain calculates, or recalculates and alters peoples mind to believe this person or people are better than they are and are superior. Which makes them feel inadequate. A lot of these mental dispositions and intimidation's, I think sometimes develop from television, movies, news stations, history, magazines, and music. However, you have to catch this mental disease at an early state and kill it before it spreads and takes over your life by limiting you. Also, by accepting you have fear and intimidation this will allow you to become more aware and realize it, then act to infiltrate the virus and disengage it before it limits your mental mega gigabyte possibilities. You must conquer fear and intimidation itself and make fear, fear you. Whatever you fear you must face it and challenge it and ultimately defeat it, because if you don't you will be forever mentally imprisoned. Once you look fear in the eyes and conquer it you will be set free! Because you have defeated your fears, intimidation's, and mental inhibitors. Remember no one is better than you and they once were where you were, so in actually that makes them just like you.

[LABELS]

Part 3

    Labels are other forms of fear and intimidation. Tittles, positions, color, society class level, stature and age all intimidates people and it has a negative impact sometimes, which keeps one extremely dependent, simple, intimidated, paralyzed, and limited to the point where people don't think for themselves and they let somebody else do it for them. However, this is not always the case, these labels and tittles also have positive influences, but in this book I am talking about the negative influence. This is what people want in positions and labels with motives to completely control you, which is to see you dependent solely upon them with no opinion. Break free from this unhealthy and digressive dependency by being creative and thinking beyond the level of what your dependency limits or allows you to think on. Someone or a group of people who have always been and still is completely dependent on others it is safe to say that they have never really dreamed for themselves. Because to dream it takes a independent thinker to dream. It is time to be independent and dream for yourself. So it's safe to say that sometimes your dreams initially were not really your dreams if you posses high levels of fear, intimidation, and dependency. They were dreams that were given to you, they were not dreams that you created or wanted to go for or dream about. Now, it's time to take charge and control of your own dreams and inspirations. Always remember to dream high and don't forget that the SKY IS THE LIMIT.

I DECLARE WAR!

(Save Yourself)

"You are not weak because you feel weak. You are weak only because you accept it to be true," (Lemon). Declaring war within yourself will break you free from fear and intimidation. Declaring war within yourself means transforming your insecurities into securities. It is transforming your weakness into strengths. Declaring war within yourself means you are going deep sea diving within yourself and when you come up, you will have uncovered things that you never knew existed. After you find those weaknesses that exist you must find the the most power you can receive, which is why these weaknesses have developed. Then you will be able to get rid of those weaknesses through finding solutions by revealing and understanding the answers to you. "When you uncover things you never thought existed, then you have salvaged the power of the gifted," (Lemon). Declaring war means you are diving into yourself with the motive to run into that great shark and that killer whale. It is facing yourself. It is facing the weakness within. Facing yourself is the most power you will ever get. The first step declaring war is gearing your focus and time on yourself. Next, one does this by getting comfortable with what makes you uncomfortable. Typically this means whatever makes you most uncomfortable, make it a personal enemy number one and a priority that you get comfortable with. One of the hardest things for people to do is travel outside their comfort zones. Because, it gives you a feeling of uneasiness, makes you uncomfortable, and gives a feeling of insecurity. "Think about it, even when you are in your comfort zone you feel insecure about certain things, so really how comfortable is your comfort zone if you don't really feel secure, safe, and at home,"(Lemon). I think one of the highest levels of insecurity is denial. We have to face and accept that this is what is causing fear and is making life uncomfortable, no meaning, unhappy, and not peaceful. You must be honest with yourself in order to fix yourself. We can never become whole and find ourselves if we do not realize what is holding us hostage. Decide and make a choice to recognize your weaknesses, accept your weaknesses, and then do not accept them by pushing toward fixing them by finding answers and solutions. Stop finding problems within others and make sure you become an archeologist of yourself. These insecurities are keeping you from finding true happiness and riches. Once you become secure with your insecurities you will gain much more happiness and peace. I think insecurities develop from mental, emotional, or a physical traumatizing past experiences that resurface and future experiences one negatively expects to happen. Which, ultimately effects our way of thinking and destroys present and future relationships. These insecurities will make us miserable, unable to love, and become unproductive. What you need not to be is what negatively, mentally, and emotionally affects you. **"People confuse their true identity with their color. But your real identity is the opposite of your deepest insecurity,"** (Lemon). Imagine focusing on turning and transforming your deepest insecurities into your most confident securities. You would be a completely different person. You will be much stronger and powerful! Your attitude and energy will be way above average and beyond what you are use too. Weakness will not be an issue or problem. Imagine your problems and issues were that you were becoming too strong as to oppose becoming weaker. Figuratively speaking, wouldn't those be great problems and issues to worry about? They say fight to the death, but you should fight to stay alive, because death is certain!

2ND PHASE

Free Your Mind

[LIBERATION]

Mind freedom is one of eight cures from mental imprisonment. The way you free your mind is being more open minded to new perspectives, new knowledge about interpretation of yourself, concepts, beliefs, truths, cultures, creeds, people, ways, positive disciplines, practices, views, rituals, foods, orientations and places. However, keeping in mind what you are opening your mind too. What you don't want to do is be counter-productive by opening your mind to more negativity and corruption. Because this will only guide you back to mental imprisonment and misery. Also still keeping your beliefs and ideals intact and standing firm on what you initially believed in and stood for, if you do not want to feel guilty about going against any prior beliefs, but still being open minded to other understandings. Which by being open to other understandings will give you different realizations that will allow you to compare and contrast your views, which ultimately will give you validation that your views are true or not. So my question is what can you lose from being open minded if you gain two or three sided to a story? Go outside of your comfort zone. This is one of the hardest things for people to do, which is going outside of their comfort zone of whatever they are use too and becoming open to new ways of and different things.

This is difficult, because people are afraid of the unknown and sometime would rather not search for something that would destroy their very identity and reality. But what if your reality is not bringing you peace and happiness? What if your reality is not giving you what you need? So, in actuality and factually your reality is already destroyed. What you just might need is to gain a better, different, and higher understanding.

Furthermore people are scared of the mysteries that change brings. However, if you are freeing your mind to positivity, then you have nothing to worry about because the mysteries will be good and benefit you. Also they would rather not explore beyond their realm of natural born taught interpretation of how life and the world is. Also most are afraid of losing themselves or a feeling of feeling as if they are betraying themselves or a higher power. However, if you are gaining more understanding through a different way and this new way gives you more peace, happiness, less stress, hate, makes you more spiritual, and brings you closer to God you are definitely on the right path of righteousness.

Compare this process of mind freeing to a job resume. So think about it this is a way to add on to your mind history as compared to adding on to your work history. Each example of adding on is an upgrade and prepares you for better opportunities in the future. Also both show that you have more understanding and more skills. So now you are more valuable and less expendable, because you now have more to offer yourself and the world.

Change is good most of the time depending how you look at it. Change is good if it makes you better, mentally healthier, stronger, more fearless, less naive, happier, more aware, and richer. However, change could be bad considering if you become more negative, miserable, mentally sicker, less financially stable and weaker. If you free you're mind you will find what you seek out and the truth will set you free. It is a way of developing a compare and contrast mindset. Freeing your mind involves doing the opposite of what you are use to. It will allow you to know the world just as much as the world knows you. I believe if you do not know how the world works, the history of it, how people work, and how the universe works how on earth can you figure out how you work? Because, you are a part of the world, people, and the universe. If you do not understand what you come from, what you are a part of, then how can you be of interest to yourself or others? Also how can you be useful, of service, an asset, or productive? You cannot change something that you have no clue of what to change.

[DELETE STEREOTYPES]

Mind freedom allows one to see past stereotypes and offers everyone the same equal opportunity. Being a person who believes in or gives into stereotypes will not offer you a free mind. It will submit you to a life of hate, ignorance, fear, and racism. Ultimately thinking stereotypical will stop you from thinking on higher levels of compassion, real truth, and understanding. Freeing your mind will give you the ability to become interchangeable and versatile, which will give you more opportunity and much higher avenues of financial stability. It will give you the ability to relate to different cultures then yours. This versatility will enable you to view the world from all angles and see the world on a broader spectrum of understanding, which will allow you to give the whole world a second chance. Having a free mind will allow you to network and communicate on different levels with a wide range of different people, religions, colors, nationalities, creeds and cultures. "Flip it, whip it, and then reverse it. Now you see things you never saw before, and now you realize there is more to life than the one you knew before,"(Lemon). Developing an open mind will allow you experience other ways besides ordinary tradition, which gives you leverage to think and be different from most people. Tradition is great sometimes, but sometimes it can become a setback in regards to powerful change by means of what's occurring now as opposed to how history was. All historical tradition is not good and should not be a pattern that the future adapts too.

[STEREOTYPES]

Part 2

For instance, if you are a car sells man and two guys come in the dealership. The first guy comes in looks a lot younger than the other and has tattoos. He has dried up paint all on his white t-shirt, shorts, and shoes. Now the next guy comes in 15 minutes after the first guy and looks older, has a fitted suit on, nice dress shoes no tattoos, and clean cut. However, the sells men ended up showing the second guy more attention off of assumption. So, the first guy left, because he didn't feel welcome. However, in actually the first guy was a multimillionaire and founder of a major construction company and was looking forward to buying a Mercedes for him and his wife. Consequently, the second guy didn't have as much money and was a local warehouse employee just window shopping. A person without a free mind will approach the second guy, because they will stereotype and go off observation instead of giving both equal opportunities. A person who does not have a free mind will not think outside the box and is simple minded and will minimize their chances of financial fortune. But, a person with a free mind will not judge people based on appearance and assumption. Fortunately this is a person who gives the world a chance and will ultimately make more money and will influence more people, because they have a broader and more versatile audience.

Think of a music artist, the ones that cater to all audiences from all walks of life are the most fortunate in money and long jeopardy, because they are versatile and interchangeable. But, in contrast artists who only attracts one particular group doesn't do as well financially, but still probably make good money, but apparently doesn't do as well as their competition. The artists who have a free mind are more original, creative, independent, unique, and stand out. Freeing your mind gives you the ability to become universal, global, and international. It guides you toward connecting to your imagination. One hit wonders don't last too long, because there mind is simple, basic, regular, usual and practical. Ultimately not having a free mind prevents one from thinking on a higher complex level. This stops people in general from having much to talk about, write about, or sing about due to a closed minded view of the world. Always be yourself! "Never try to mimic or copy someone else, because you are not being original, you are being artificial. You can copy a cat, but you cannot copy its scent, so there is no use to follow in its footprints," (Lemon).

(INDEPENDENCY)

Uniqueness

Freeing your mind gives you in-dependency, uniqueness, and sets you apart from the rest. "Originality takes work, self-improvement, transcending, and the capability to separate yourself from commonality," (Lemon). Think about it like this in this order, commonality, capability, and then originality. In other words when you realize that you are common and the same as everyone else then you now have the power to understand that you are much more capable to be better then what makes you just like everybody else. Ultimately the next step is to work on yourself and self-improve toward originality. Originality blesses you with the ability to think on your own and make decisions based on your intuition. Freeing your mind develops you into a leader. Don't be a follower be a leader! Freeing your mind will enable you to think on a leadership level. Thinking on a leadership level gives you the opportunity to make more money. So, to say the least by acquiring that mindset it is only safe to say your job title and position will soon change, which your life will change as well. For example later, you will move up sooner than you ever expected, (which you never expected originally due to your prior isolated closed minded mindset) and ultimately becoming a supervisor, manager, general manager, and CEO of that company or another one and maybe your own. Mind freedom allows one to develop immunity from stereotyping people and sets them free from mental racism and segregationalism. For example, just like the saying, never judge a book by its cover. This is the mindset you will develop once gaining a freed mind. You will see everyone as equal no matter what color, shape, size, culture, religion or creed. Ultimately a person with a free mind will take you beyond average success, because you adopted a view that allows you to give everyone a chance. You will cater to everyone no matter who they are and they will show you the same love.

[INTELLIGENCE]

I have only four definitions that I speak on from a range of much more intelligences that are produced by freeing your mind. My first definition of intelligence is one being when someone can be extremely productive within a given unproductive environment and turn that unproduction into production. My next definition of intelligence is when a person actually feels the understanding that they are mentally learning. "It is a huge difference between learning and understanding as opposed to actually feeling the understanding that you are learning," (Lemon). Another definition of intelligence is when people can communicate on different levels and relate to anyone within any environment or any walk of life. My last definition of intelligence comes from a professional sports point of view (NBA, NFL, MLB, NHL, etc). These players perform at a very high level of discipline, focus, and concentration. My last definition of a form of intelligence is when you can perform at a very high level of pressure, humiliation, stress, criticism, and worry. But yet still focusing, concentrating, maintaining confidence and gaining victory! This is extreme focus intelligence.

[GENIUSES]

"Our biggest fear is not what we see, but it is what our curiosity has the possibility to be," (Lemon). Mind freedom brings the genius out of you. If your curiosity leads to you gaining a better understanding of yourself, your gifts, the genius in you, better interpretation of knowledge, and the world, then never stop asking questions. Mind freedom frees your curiosity and power, then your curiosity creates creativity and creativity creates geniuses and uniqueness. This freedom and power creates geniuses, great scientists, and inventors such as Granville T. Woods, Jan Matzeliger, Madam Walker, Patricia Bath, and Albert Einstein. They are complex thinkers to the point where most people couldn't understand their thought process. Because, their thought process processed on different levels due to a freed mind. These people with great minds of genius only became great because they finally accepted the fact that they were great. Anyone can be a genius; you just have to find a unique way to bring it out of you and realize you posses such abilities. The way to genius is through the process of freeing your mind, which will develop your creativity through feeding your curiosity.

"The huge difference between smart, intelligent, and wise people as opposed to those without these abilities is they make sure they create time to dedicate themselves to thinking,"(Lemon). Also it is a huge difference between having a great memory as opposed to understanding what you remember. You must put your mind on an exercise program. For example, comparable to lifting weights and exercising. For instance, after you are done exercising your body gets stronger, muscles develop; get more complex, and well defined. This is how the brain feels as if it were exercising and developing or finally utilizing more brain cells, while processing information at a rapid pace. We must realize that the way we think determines how are life will be spiritually, mentally, emotionally, physically, and financially. "Originality means that you go back to the foundation of your existence and you bring out your true self," (Lemon).

(SENSES ARE NOT SO COMMON)

"Gaining higher senses allows you to stand out from the count of the census," (Lemon). I think people misuse the phrase common sense. We criticize those who we think should know certain things when in fact they are not at that level of sense. However, we unintentionally humiliate those who we tell, "this is common sense." However, this is not common sense to them, because they do not have that level of sense as I stated before. By telling someone this is common sense and they do not understand it puts extreme negative pressure on their mind. Because they are trying to understand something that is far beyond their mind and on another level of understanding but cant, which puts them in a situation of extreme vulnerability, pressure, humiliation, and high levels of confusion. Common sense is only common if it makes sense to that individual. You are insulting a level of sense that they do not occupy. So, if you think about it who is the one who is not displaying common sense, you or them? Also it is only common sense if that person understands every aspect of that commonality on that level of sense. For example, a brain surgeon who is operating on a patient. This doctor has an assistant and tells the assistant to grab an instrument and puncture the frontal lobe. Then, "she says I don't know how." Then, the surgeon says, "This is common sense." We all know this is not common sense to the assistant. Because, these two people have very two different levels of knowledge, information, training, and experience. They are both trained and specialize at two different levels of sense and understanding. I look at sense being forms of intelligence. Everyone can acquire high levels of sense, you just have to take your mind beyond what's considered common to you. Typically speaking you must reach different levels of sense by learning more than you generally know. I don't categorize sense any longer as being common. Because everyone has different levels of sense, so it becomes not so common does it?

[YOUR ENVIRONMENT DOES NOT DETERMINE YOUR EXPERIENCE]

Another freedom of freeing your mind gives you the ability to think and go outside what you naturally were born into. People wonder why their life has not changed; it is because your mind has not changed. Your life will only be lead towards the direction that your mind is thinking. You will only be guided down the path of which your perception allows you to understand. It is a saying that states, you are a product of your environment. But, I disagree, "Your mind and how you think determines what environment you will be a product of," (Lemon). It is your choice after you figure out that your environment is a huge factor controlling and determining how you view the world, people, how you will think, how you will live, and who you will be. You must think outside of your environment in order to understand that thinking in it is what made you become it. Your environment represents what society expects you to be and society does not expect you to be anything beyond what you were suppose to accept to be. "Think past what your environment does not encourage you to focus on and what society does not expect you to be," (Lemon). You will be successful and you will become what you want to be, but only if you do not allow yourself to worry about what others do not expect you to be. There is life and knowledge outside of your natural born environment, which will give you more control over what you want to focus on, how you want to be, what you want to learn, where you want to go and end up. Your habitat is referred to as environmental. Because your environment affects your mental state of mind and your environment develops your habits. Break your pattern of habits by forcing yourself to think beyond your environment. Also for example, if you live in an environment where you are not exposed to or you do not see a habit of success, happiness, and wealth, then this is what you focus on and get into the habit of becoming. "The one's who adapt to their environment, but still remain masters of their behavior, see the world beyond what their environment projected them to experience,"(Lemon).

[ORDER]

"If you do not occasionally change the pattern and routine of order, then you will never be able to develop new and higher realms of consciousness," (Lemon). Freeing your mind gives you the power to change distorted and destructive forms of order. God supports order, but righteous order is what God backs up with divine power. I believe some order, rules, and laws do not protect you they actually restrict you from being what God intended us all to be, which is free, great, and powerful. There has always has to be boundaries, but when these boundaries limit others from happiness, higher knowledge, and power to control their own lives, then this is a order that must be revised. Sometimes you learn the most and find the most knowledge when you get out the order of things that you typically are in. Ultimately when you free you're mind you will possess the ability to see and realize the big picture in regards to the order you were in before. Which you will be able to recognize if this order was the reason why you were out of order and out of control in the first place. "Fix your thinking pattern by breaking it," (Lemon). Meaning in order to think different and gain different levels of knowledge you must think outside your pattern of comfortability and natural born order of perspectives and understanding.

"Once you stop doing the same thing, then you will realize you was the reason for not accomplishing your dreams," (Lemon). When you free your mind you will be able to think outside of the history of your limited knowledge. Sometime people rely too much on history to scope the future. For example, if a family has a history of heart disease, if someone somewhere down the line doesn't alter this historic fatal disease it will continue to plaque each generation to quicker fatalities. So, in different cases it's a positive and healthy thing not sticking to historic tradition. Times change, people change, places change, everything evolves. Your mind has to evolve if it doesn't your mind will be stuck in history and your body will be living in the future. So in reality your mind will become history! The only thing that doesn't change and stays historic tradition is the will and destiny of the creator. This mindset of freedom will give the ability to gain uniqueness about you. Anything unique gets more attention and people will develop a desire to learn more about it. When people desire to learn something they tend to admire whatever it is they are learning and whoever it is that is teaching. This mentality will lead you to a great career in teaching, millionaire financial planners, presidents, innovators, presidential advisers, presidential spokeswomen and men, mentoring, great millionaire marketers, promoters, billionaire realtors, global motivational speakers, etc.

Freeing your mind will indeed lead to financial success as I just gave a prime example of developing into a leader and attracting people through developing uniqueness. Anyone who can persuade those into the lucrative business of persuasion will gain great fortune. However, persuade people for the right reasons that will lead them to happiness, peace, and fortune. As opposed to having bad motives and negative intentions which will lead them toward unhappiness and misfortune. This theory is proven time and time again through historic and current examples such as old world Emperors, Kings, and Queens of good and bad motives and intentions. So, you should learn from history and realize history repeats itself if the future opportunity presents itself. Current examples of people gaining fortune through unique mind freedom, which gave them power of persuasion to accumulate people are men and women like Aliko Dangote, Oprah Winfrey, Donald Trump, **Lakshmi Mittal, Carlos Slim Helu and Sheldon Aldenson, Christy Walton,**

Bill Gates, and Liliane Bettencourt and plenty others. These men and women are all Billionaires.

Ultimately freeing your mind gives you better navigational skills through life and what obstacles it may bring. This gift allows you to be more investigative, and more mentally financially business savvy. Also you become more open and receptive to what and who is around you. You will be more inviting to all no matter what age, culture or color.

Mind freedom will eventually give you the gift of gaining insight and giving everyone a chance based upon character and not color. Ultimately, you will uncover and discover things you would never even have the ideas and thoughts to think about if you never developed a freed mind. You will become more of a listener and more compassionate and understanding to each individual situation. Your mind will go to a higher level of complex thinking. A freed mind of freedom gives you the power of creativity to say the least. By having the power of creativity you are freer than most, because you are not bound by the restrictions and perimeters of common order. I believe a person with a free mind alone will bring them much fortune, because you are a person who does not fall victim to forced perspectives and ways of being.

3RD PHASE

Develop a Strong Mindset

[SELF-INTELLECT]

"ONCE YOU GAIN KNOWLEDGE, THEN YOU DO NOT HAVE TO BELIEVE IN LUCK ANYMORE," (Lemon). Developing a strong mindset and self-intellect is another vital need for curing mental imprisonment. You must gain knowledge in order to bring more choices and opportunities to you. Doesn't it make sense, how could you think by not having any knowledge beyond what stops you from being success and happy that you will be successful and happy? One develops a strong mind through self-intellect. The way you gain self thinking is a simple strategy of being open minded to learning and attaining more and new knowledge and information through yourself to the point where your mind will be enhanced to higher mental intellectual levels of your own consciousness. Remember the saying, "Knowledge is Power" this is certain and a factual statement. I believe self-knowledge is even more powerful, because self-knowledge blesses you with self-wisdom. Wisdom gives you power and vision beyond ignorance.

The more you use your brain and mind for you, and the more you think, the more money you will make, and the more ways you will know of how to make yourself happy. Overall self-complex thinking is a way to elevate your intellect and to activate and stimulate more brain cells then you are accustomed too. It's time to accomplish yourself! Put your mind to you. "You cannot accomplish anything that you never thought to put your mind too nor can you put your mind to anything that you can not think about," (Lemon). Its time to step your thinking game up! You are not doing yourself any justice by not understanding your true potential. The only way to realize your true potential is by thinking toward it. It's time to put your focus and mind on you! It's time to electrify and stimulate your brain cells and mind, because this is the only way not to fail! In my opinion when one develops this power there is a 100 percent guarantee of happiness, peace, financial success and fortune beyond your wildest dreams.

[NEW PERCEPTION/ NEW EXPERIENCE]

NEW FREEDOM!

"The more knowledge you obtain, the more information you retain, then the more freedom you gain. Which means the higher you will be above lower level systems of control," (Lemon).Give yourself a chance to accumulate more options by deciding to free your mind through new perspectives and perceptions about the world, you, and other people. Ultimately these new perceptions will expand your mind with new powerful knowledge and information. Which will give you more freedom and put you above lower levels of systems of control. In addition this freedom of control will develop new opportunities and choices. The more options and choices create more confidence. I compare living in a lower level system of control to focus and time. What I mean by lower level systems of control is when all your focus and time is controlled by everything and everyone but you. You might as well be in a prison, because you do not control any aspect of your life, because your focus and time is not geared toward what you want to do. You cannot be happy or feel fulfilled if everything is in control of you but you. Your focus and time is a representation of your life, you, who you are, and what you will become. How could you have ever really found out who you are if you never geared any of your focus and time toward yourself? In addition everything that is controlling your focus and time half the time are not things that give you peace and happiness and are not things you desire to do. It is a huge difference between when your focus and time is consumed by everything that you do not desire and want to do as opposed to most of your focus and time being controlled by everything that you love to do, have a passion to do, and what brings you peace, and happiness. Which if your time is controlled by things that give you happiness, then really there is nothing controlling you, because there is no fight. When there is no fight, then that is complete happiness. At this level you see your focus and time giving you freedom and accomplishment, instead of controlling you and making you feel inadequate and unaccomplished. When you control your focus and a lot of your time you have true freedom. You will have a different attitude and energy level when you can focus on things that make you happy, passionate, and accomplished. You will be more positive and more confident. For example, I believe this is why a lot of movie stars, athletes, singers, have a different attitude, energy, and bring a different conversation. I'm sure they all still go through there times of despair. But I am making an example of how they are or anybody above lower levels of systems of control, because their focus and time is being consumed by what they want to do, makes them happy, confident, and gives them a higher sense of freedom. However, you do not have to be a movie star, singer, or sports player to achieve this freedom. You just have to take the time out to gain more control back over your focus and time by doing things that makes you happy, fill whole, gives you a sense of purpose, makes you confident and peaceful. "Nobody can make any decisions that are more intelligent and sophisticated then their limited options," (Lemon). If you have limited options, most likely you cannot make any smart and confident decisions past what you can see, understand, or what you can not perceive. With new perception comes higher level of knowledge, better intelligent decision making skills, and broader range of options and opportunities. Which this new perception will give you the insight to make confident decisions that you will benefit from and will go your way.

New perceptions set's you free from what you never could see and sets you free from what could see you, but you could never see it. It reveals the unseen. The price of freedom is the truth. However, once you get it you receive more power and control over your life. Which these new perceptions and new truths gives you the power to accumulate more opportunity and choices beyond lower systems of control. "Either your perception will lead you to self-destruct or it will build you up," (Lemon). You broaden your perception by gaining higher levels of knowledge, information, and more mentally healthier experiences. The more you know yourself, the more you know you will find out what makes you happy, and the more you will realize what is your passion. The less you know about yourself, the less knowledge and information you will have to know about making you happy and surer. Also the more you know yourself, the more you will know where you need to go, the more options/choices you will have, and the more you will know how to lead yourself on the right path. "No one can make any decisions that are beyond their limited given perspective and actually know and be in control of the outcome," (Lemon). To be a much better you, you must gain higher perspectives, which will put you in better positions to control the results of what you can now see at the level of. You gain higher levels of perception by tapping into yourself and redefining how you collect data internally (inside view) and externally (outside view). The more knowledge, more options, the more choices, more control, and more confidence. The more options are limited, the less choices, which generates limited control over your destiny.

"Your predictions of your future will not fall below the present strength you are living in unless you become distracted by your old self," (Lemon). Sometimes you must change your perception for purposes to go toward the direction of strength. What you want is to breathe and live strength. Even your last breath before you die will even be a breath that is stronger than any breaths you took before you made a commitment toward strength. Sometimes you must change you perception in order to reach your informational and intellectual levels. Sometimes you have to think beyond what you know in order to find out what you need to know. We must find out ways and reach perceptions that will give us more peace, freedom, and happiness.

"Go against everything that makes you weak and even go against what you know if that is the root of your weakness,"(Lemon).

(PUT YOUR PERSPECTIVE TO THE TEST)

Some institutions have good intentions, but I believe take a lot of teachings out of context. Which creates false and distorted knowledge, or limited knowledge and understanding of what they are actually teaching. This produces misinterpretation and a follower to be misinformed and misguided. Ultimately this teaching that is taken out of context inevitably becomes teachings to the followers that are way below the perspective and concepts of what actually should be taught from the text. So in reality this puts them so far from higher understanding and knowledge of what they in actuality really should be learning, studying, practicing, and living. Which this creates a trickle down effect that limits their experience, happiness, peace, freedom, power, destiny, opportunities, choices, and ultimately life. In addition this limited knowledge and understanding through being taught through misinterpretation and text taken out of context prevents even the teacher let alone the students from asking the right questions or receiving the right answers toward what really should be taught, studied, and practiced. Put your perspective to the test! If you gain higher knowledge and understanding by going outside of your perspective then and only then you can be the judge of your own perspective. That is what you want, which is an outside view of your own view and understanding. "You cannot be taught a powerful way, the right way, ask the right questions, or get the right answers within a perspective that limits your knowledge and understanding,"(Lemon).

TRUE LEADERS

(Visionaries)

Self-complex intellect turns you into a true leader and visionary. True leaders are followers just as everyone is in the beginning and when leaders they still are followers,but the difference now is they have direction. But they break free from high levels of co-dependence and irresponsibility. They follow and become extremely disciplined in a strict set of codes and guidelines. **"Anybody who stands for something great will always be presented with conflict, not because they are presenters of conflict, but because they will not etiquettely sit down,"**(Lemon). They make commitments and oaths that they don't even allow themselves to break. Which allows them to possess a higher level of belief and practice. True leaders become their beliefs. I believe beliefs in itself give you a purpose to live. Leader's posses' true belief, to live is to believe! True believe is practice. A true leader a lot of times does not rely on facts when setting goals, dreams, and visions. A true leader is a dreamer and doer. They take action. Dreaming and using their imagination is how they break through and look past the circumstances and what they see. These special types of people develop a higher connection to the truth. Which that truth opens their mind to power! This power allows them to break through many mental levels of restraint and limitation. This sets them apart from followers. For example, what is false to a follower is true to a leader, what is impossible is highly possible to a leader, and what is fake to a follower is more likely real to a leader. This is how much of an informational and perceptional gap there is between a follower and a leader. This is how a leader can become a visionary and a follower can only see at the level they are told to see. Become a leader then you will find out what it means to use your imagination. Leaders are set apart by their individuality. "It is not where you are from, or who you know. It is about what you know, what you were taught, and how you can use what you know to scope and create your own individualism," (Lemon).

WHAT INFLUENCED YOU TO BECOME YOU?

(Experience Yourself)
Reflective Focusing

Experiencing yourself is another powerful way to again self-intellect. Focusing on reflecting creates a deep meditative self empowering experience lead by your memory to travel as a tour guide through your mind with specifically focusing on the creation of your mental development giving full attention to all adolescent and teenage influences by means of gaining internal data and information for purposes of achieving a better understanding of one's self. Once you understand yourself, then you have the ability to change yourself. If you do not understand yourself, then everybody else has the power to influence and mold you how they want you without taken in consideration how you would want or need to be. Ultimately without understanding yourself you would not have a clue as to what you really need and how you should be. Reflective focusing is compared to reflective psychology. It is a way to track how your memory and way of thinking has developed over large periods of time. You could say reflective focusing is a thinking tracking device that is lead by your memory. Another definition of reflective focusing is deep reminiscing processes taking in regard everything that you could possibly remember to think about when gaining data on how you became you.

"It becomes a miracle and is amazing how much knowledge and wisdom one will gain by just understanding who they really are as opposed to what they were not meant to become," (Lemon). Remember you are your memory, so knowing the history of your memory will allow you to unravel the history of you. Everyone through this journey of life will have many experiences, in which we gain understanding and wisdom through them. However do you ever hear people say that one of the best experiences that they had was themselves? Your experiences influence the person you become. By understanding what influenced you to become you will give you the power to understand how you became you, how your mind was developed, and will give you the power to gain back the control of influence over yourself. "If you stop to think to put your mind under surveillance. You would be surprised to find out how many security breaches you were subjected too," (Lemon).

Experiencing yourself means to realize who you are. You cannot gain any experience from something you never gave your focus and time too. Meaning to gain a much clearer understanding of yourself, you must experience yourself by directing your focus and time to yourself. "You are not alive until you have experienced your true potential of how great you can be," (Lemon). For example, not ever experiencing yourself is compared to writing your own book, but you cannot understand your own writing. But those who read your book understands your book more than you do. This is backwards. How can you know who you are, if you do not know or understand what is inside you?

HIGHER EXPERIENCE OF YOU

(Find the Solution to You)

When you have a problem and you solve your own problem and find a solution to your own problem, this means you are self-developing and self-improving at a very rapid pace. Self-development leads to higher experiences of you. These higher experiences of yourself will surely guide you toward trusting yourself and your intuition more than leaning on bad advice and misdirected guidance from outsiders. Self-development for example is like being eleven in 6th grade and skipping from elementary to high school. It is a faster way toward knowledge, which gives you a deeper understanding and wisdom of yourself. I am not saying isolate yourself from everybody and do not ask for advice or guidance. However, when you get advice or guidance, by already self-developing you will know from within if this guidance or advice will benefit you or not. Because if it doesn't sit well with your inner self and you know you would make a better decision by taking your own advise why would you make the mistake to make a decision based off of someone else's logic.

(THE BLUE PILL OR THE RED PILL)

Within the movie the Matrix Morpheus gave Neo the option of taking the red or the blue pill. Which by taking either would lead him into different directions. Taking the blue pill would send him back to his life within the matrix, which he would stay the same, believe the same beliefs, and would not get any closer toward the power of why. However, the red pill would lead him out of captivity, toward salvation, out of the matrix, and gaining power of why. Neo took the red pill, which gave him the power of asking the right questions toward higher awareness and consciousness. Take the red pill, so you can gain the power of why of yourself. You cannot come up with any solutions if you do not know the right questions to ask. When you gain higher understanding of yourself, then you will form the right questions, which you will find the solutions. The more questions you come up with regarding yourself, just in question alone you have reached higher thoughts of power of experiencing yourself. The power is within the questions. By coming up with powerful questions about yourself will only lead you toward gaining ultimate power within yourself. When you answer your own questions those answers will become your solutions to yourself. Ultimately answering and finding your own solutions will answer your why questions. By answering your own questions will connect you to a much higher consciousness, brain development, perception, and are reaching a higher more powerful you. By going deep inside yourself you will find your answers and solutions to you. When you find the answers to the why questions of you, these powerful answers will lead to solutions, which these answers that lead to solutions are a process to experience a better more powerful you. Ultimately this self experience through developing answers to your problems will lead to solutions that will enable you to heal yourself, your own mind, body, soul, and spirit. Ultimately this process will allow you to continue to disconnect from mental imprisonment toward gaining mental immortality.

4ᵀᴴ PHASE

(Develop a Strong Heart)

When I say develop a strong heart throughout this book I do not mean heart as in the organ. I refer to the heart as our will power! Our will power fuels our spirit, will, confidence, and drive! How do you know how much you can handle if you never knew how much you could take? You cannot know your true potential if you never pushed yourself to the limit. Developing a strong heart you must develop more strength, endurance, discipline, practice, and a stronger spirit! Also when I refer to a strong heart I mean by developing strong will power and spirit will help you generate positive will fighting emotions. It will help you fight negative emotions of defeat, depression, unhappiness, unsuccess, and turmoil. Developing a strong heart is one of the most essential ways and strategies of gaining internal happiness, peace and financial success. Ways of developing a strong heart is being open minded and susceptible to all criticism, whether constructive or deconstructive. Letting your guard down and being on the offense instead of the defense. To do this you must set your pride aside and listen and learn from your own faults. This will allow you to realize your weakness and individual personal setbacks. If you think about it weakness are not positive, because they are setbacks. I believe weaknesses are inconsistencies that develop through lack of discipline, practice, confidence, and concentration. It is not from the light of empowerment and strength. You have to build up your heart (your fight) with positivity, strength, discipline, and endurance. The last step after realizing and accepting your weaknesses is to turn your weaknesses into your strengths. Turning your weakness into strengths allows you to defeat all fear, intimidations, and insecurities. You must declare war on all your inconsistencies. I believe our heart (also I refer to as our will power) really defines us as a human species. Also it gives a spark of determination and inspiration through termination. Eventually the setbacks of the world will only give you fuel to do well. If you never experienced suffering and major setbacks how could you know how strong you really are?

Implementing these practices will build your heart and make you stronger: 1. being open minded and susceptible to all criticism, whether constructive or destructive 2. All negativity directed toward you turn positive 3.letting your guard down and being on the offense instead of the defense. Implementing these practices within your life will help you develop a strong heart to deal with life's curve balls. Also adopting these strategies will build character and will make you into a strong warrior, soldier, queen and king. We were all proclaimed and destined to be these great legendary strong humans of honor and integrity. The point of developing a strong heart is to be much better prepared for the storms and setbacks that will come your way down the line. When you develop this power you won't break down easy. Ultimately people that think their breaking you down is only building you up, because you are now turning your weaknesses into strengths. Whatever those initially tried to break you down with, you will consider what they said and use it to reanalyze yourself and fix what they initially tried to criticize you for.

You must develop a strong heart for strength and fight, so when you go through life you will not allow negative emotions become your downfall by allowing it to hunt you and destroy your strength and spirit. These negative emotions can and will be something from your past that was traumatic to you whether physical trauma, mental trauma but most damaging physical and mental trauma together. Also, these emotions will make you miserable and weak. This will present you with a life of vulnerability if you allow it too. This is where your heart being strong with fight of Lion and strength of a bear will come in handy. This level of fight will ensure victory, strength, and happiness! However, it's not some peoples fault, sometimes bad thing happens to people at a young age that they cannot control or really understand until they reach an age where they can and that memory never left. But, now they understand what transpired and don't know a positive constructive way to deal with it. The main cure is facing this mental monster and striping it off its powers over you. In addition ultimately forgiveness is a quicker way towards your recovery. You will defeat this monster when you realize you gave it strong power by allowing it to feed on you. Then ultimately generating negative emotions that submitted you to feel fear, shame, hatred, and guilt.

Once one tap into positive emotions and feelings this will enable one to not feel these negative emotions of shame, guilt and fear and will conquer this monster. People give these negative these monsters too much power through conscious and subconscious avenues of misery. What you must realize is that you cannot run from these monsters no matter how far or how fast you run, from going to another country to another continent. So how do you defeat this inhibitor? First you have to accept that is a life detrimental issue that you continue to give power too, which makes you feel vulnerable. One must realize first that there is a problem and this is the first step to recovery, peace, happiness. Then, you must maintain a positive mindset and defeat this by tapping into your good positive emotions such as being happy, gladness, joy, cheer, forgiveness, and peace. Also other means of support and guidance. Which these positive emotions will produce positive concepts and thoughts. Which will ultimately positively affect your spirit and fight, will, and give you power to be happy.

Motivation Resuscitation!

The Doubters?

The Doer's!

THE DOUBTERS?

Negative Wanderers

Once you gain and retain a strong confident mindset you will form a type of immunity toward negative people who doubt you and already have in their clogged minds negative thoughts and concepts about you. So what good will it do you to be around people who doubt you and have such retribution and corrupted thoughts about you? When you develop a strong confident positive clear thinking mind you will be able to feel all the hate, doubt, and negativity people have festered up in their miserable minds and hearts about you. You will now be able to see through people and how they feel about you through their body language, eyes, energy, and conversation. So you will now be prepared for their words of negativity and it will not disrupt your new found peace, dreams, and positive thinking. You will realize what you never once saw from people that swear they love you; you will see how negative their views are about you through their words of communication to you.

Ultimately everything they say is with negativity. Furthermore, obviously this negative mindset is implanted within their minds and deeply rooted within their hearts, spirits, and souls. Also, you will see the agony and despair and doubt within their soul through their eyes of pain, hurt, animosity, and unhappiness. You will now know these people you are not to tell your dreams and inspirations to, because they will discourage you through their eyes and words of doubt and will take you as a joke and not take you serious. Ultimately, they won't even have to say a word and you have already read them and felt their negative spirit and soul. Now you will then know what these people think of you and have always thought of you from your teenage years to adulthood, whether it be family, friends, associates or coworkers. Then you will be more mentally aware of the people who never really cared about you and never the less loved you. However, don't have hate and hold grudges or preserve animosity towards them, forgive these people and move on and maintain peace, happiness, and harmony despite those who wish upon you defeat and despair, because of how their life is going and will end up if they never change their mindset. They are called HATERS! Big ups to all my haters. Haters keep you motivated and confident. They see you doing something different that they do not have the confidence to do, so they will hate and make comments, but this is how you realize they just want to be just like you, but are jealous because they can't.

NEGATIVE WANDERERS

"The doubters are the people who will say you are too arrogant, just to try to bring you down to their level of low confidence, encouragement, and competence,"(Lemon). The doubters are the ones who cannot do what you do, because they doubt what they do, so they will never believe in you. These are the people who do not truly believe, because their hope is guided by doubt and they lack true faith. These are the people who question everything they do and will surely question and doubt everything you do. These people are the ones who give up before they even try. So really they just ultimately prove their doubtful state of mind right about themselves. I respect a person for at least going for their dreams and trying, rather than a person who never tried at all. For example, I wanted to become a radiographer (x-ray tech). I knew it was a challenge receiving admittance into such a high demand career. These instructors of the program wanted the best, so they accepted applicants according to high G Pa's. Apparently the ones with low G Pa's had a very low chance of acceptance. So, I pushed myself past what I originally expected of myself and developed much higher expectation. Ultimately I received admittance. My point is I tried my best, took the risk of losing not failing. So, I experienced this dream I had and decided it was not what I was passionate about, so in reality it was not my true dream or purpose. But, I went for it, got it, but didn't want it. Which is nothing wrong with that decision. At least I got the opportunity and experience to realize this was something I wasn't passionate about. It's a saying that I hold dear too, "better to have loved, then never loved at all."

Sometimes you have to re-dream your own dreams and construct a purpose you created and not depend on a purpose somebody else made up for you. Because, if you do not do well in that purpose you will feel like a failure. However, you are not a failure, because that was just not your true purpose or calling. If you make your own purpose nobody can take that away from you and you will never fail at it. I gave it my all and I did it against all odds. When in reality the only odds there was, were the ones I created. I believe the only odds that are against you are the ones you make yourself. I do not believe in luck, you make your own luck! So, do not use anything as a excuse or clutch to stop yourself from becoming great and doing great things. Because you will begin to doubt yourself and think others are better than you when you have not even given yourself a chance. What you need to do is be better than yourself. Everybody told me how much competition I was facing to receive acceptance within the program. They told me how hard it would be to get in. Everyone told me how much work it would be. This type of advice is counter productive and permits a chance of doubt. As if I need to hear what I already know. They never told me I can and will do it. They never once said it's a challenge, but you'll conquer it. They never said this level of sense that you have to get to will be common and easy for you. Also, when I received admittance within the program people still doubted my completion of it. These people were the doubters. Do not look at what competition is ahead just think ahead of the competition. Never think within the past and reminisce about bad negative past experiences. Furthermore, never think ahead within the future and expect the worst, because both frames of mind develop doubt and fear. But always prepare for the future, but never think in despair of the future. So my point is do not listen, focus on, or take advice from doubters. Never think how hard something will be, because you will develop self doubt. Just think of the ways you can make it easier. Just go into it and give it your best and don't compare yourself to anyone but yourself. Because in the end if you lose, you still gave it your best and that is honorable.

"You get some of the most valuable advice from those who know and accept their faults from admitting their failures as opposed to those who deny their weaknesses," (Lemon). What can you truly learn from people who refuse to attend to their weaknesses? What you can learn is not to be like that. The strong go and search for their weaknesses, then turn them into strengths. Now they can tell you how not to be weak from admitting they had some. Ultimately you will gain the luxury of not having to go through so much weakness, because you have gained wisdom from the strongest, which are the ones who conquer their weakness first by admitting they had them. I think people confuse losing with failure. In my opinion losing is something honorable and respectable if you gave it your all. However, failing is something dishonorable because you didn't give it your all or didn't even try, so you failed, because you didn't give yourself a fair chance to lose.

"If you know what it means to fail, then you understand what it takes to succeed," (Lemon). Never think about the competition before yourself proclaimed mission, because you are giving them the power and might develop self doubt. Once you enter the competition if you see yourself falling behind or losing, this is the time to regroup and restrategize. First believe in yourself and your initial strategy before changing it, because why change something if it working. If you see it not working, then retract and react to fix your mistakes and get back in the competition and win. The doubters are not the risk takers. These are the people who do not take risks and will tell you that your risk is too risky. The doubters are the people who run and hide from a challenge. These are the people you do not want to be around if you are a doer. Doubters and negative wanderers will try to bring down your level of confidence if you allow them too. Which they will eventually have you doubting yourself. Never doubt yourself! These people are the ones who think so much about failing that failing becomes normal and suspected for them and others. So they in turn do not believe that you have what it takes to succeed, because they did not. So being around doubters will only bring you down and back track you toward retreat and defeat.

[THE DOER'S!]

Believers

"Those who are successful do not let mistakes define who they are, but rather allow their mistakes redefine what they must do," (Lemon).Once you stop taking risks you stop dreaming and once you stop dreaming you stop living. Ambition, determination, and motivation without knowledge is just a dream. The doers dream as well as gain knowledge, so they can take control of their dreams by turning them into realities. The doer's are the knowledgeable dreamers. You cannot take action on a dream and desire and expect to turn it into a reality without gaining knowledge. I don't hope anymore. I gain knowledge and make it happen and take action! You cannot overcome any circumstance by just hoping to get out. All of that hope that you using to get out you could be spending that focus and time preparing plan to get out. The doer's do, they do not try.

"Take trying out of your vocabulary, because, all it is doing is stunting what is necessary," (Lemon).

You never hear people who survived against all odds, who survived a hurricane, or get out tragic events by saying I tried to live. No they did live by forcing themselves to breath above death. The doer's are the ones you need to be around for motivation and inspiration. However, you must not look for people to give you encouragement all the time, because the most important encouragement is within yourself. But it does help to be among people who are positive and encouraging. Because sometime everyone lose enthusiasm, so it is good to be around people who will be like a back-up engine of determination. Also the doers and believers will help you to maintain confident and enthusiastic conversation. Never doubt yourself, because once you doubt yourself and slip into a doubt coma this is when you lose control over your life and dreams. "You have to think outside of the struggle and make the struggle, struggle to keep up with you and not you struggling to keep up with the struggle," (Lemon). You will never get ahead if you are still behind it. You must get in front of it so it will remain in your past and your future will be greatness and prosperity.

The doer's are the ones who turn dreams into reality. "My motto is you have think past a galaxy off into the infinity." (Lemon). The doubters are the ones who stay in their limited reality of simplicity. "The doer's go beyond a simple reality and recreate a reality of complexity." (Lemon). The doer's take action, but the doubters settle for low satisfaction. The doubters push it to the limit, but the doer's push it past the limit. The doubters pout, but the doer's live in clout. It is not good to be a doer and be around a doubter, because a doer is mentally high with motivation, but a doubter is mentally low and sedated. The doer's keep their heads high, but the doubters keep their heads low and the only time they raise them is when they have something negative to say. The doer's are the leaders and the doubters are the negative wanderers. Which one are you?

The doer's cannot follow the doubters, because it will only lead back to doubter ship. It will only lead to circles of despair. This is why you cannot stay around doubters for long periods of time, because for this inadequate and unproductive period of time you are around them, they will doubt you, which you will be susceptible to begin doubting yourself again. So, you could have spent that time around fellow doer's who would've up lifted you and mentally elevated you. "BELIEVE IN YOURSELF AND THINK PAST YOURSELF TO MAKE YOURSELF LIVE UP TO A BETTER YOU," (Lemon). I don't agree to this quote in every case, "Be All You Can Be." I say, "Be more than you can be, because being all you can be sometimes just isn't enough," (Lemon).I say this because, what if all you can be is not what you are capable of being. I say this because what if all some can be was a failure and disappointment because that was their fate and destiny through an inherited negative mindset also known as a destructive and unproductive way of thinking. Also a failure could be what they were projected to become, because of were they were placed, what environment they were inherited, or what they were born into. Which they for the most part only will do what they know. Because initially they had no other choice, because that is all they really know, this is the only way they know how to think based upon their given perspectives of the world and themselves. Nobody can be responsible or take control over a situation that they never was taught how to get out of. I believe the saying "when you know no better you do no better." However, if you change your negative perspectives, you will reverse this destiny of failure and despair, which will enable you to become a doer and a leader!

The doubters are the ones who think so much before taking a risk that they trick themselves into doubting themselves. Don't get me wrong there are always smarter ways of evaluating risks before taking them. But, after evaluating that risk, what is stopping you from taking it? You are stopping you from taking it. The doers are optimistic and take the risk. Life is a risk to live in itself. To really live means you take risks to find out how it feels to be alive! "If you think about it, you are better off taking a risk, because it is much more riskier to not take that risk considering that you will have to deal with the future thought, memory, and regret of not taking that risk,"(Lemon). Self doubt is a negative emotion that stops us from greatness. You must defeat self doubt, and then you will soar higher than an eagle. When you look down you will see the doubters of despair and fly among the doer's of high in contaminated fresh air.

[STOP DOUBTING YOURSELF]

"If your level of doubt supersedes your level of confidence, then you will never experience the power of true believers," (Lemon) Once you stop doubting yourself, mentally you are already rich, now you must turn this mindset into a physical manifestation, which is money. I believe the pursuit and journey towards money and riches is a physical representation of what resembles the drive, motivation, determination, and inspiration we all have inside. "Knowledge is the true lottery ticket, and cash is just a reminder of how much you know," (Lemon). There is nothing wrong with wanting to be rich or the pursuit of money. However, make money, but never let money make you. Money does not give you power, you give money power. Never let money control you and become the only reason you are alive. Because once it's gone and when or if you lose it, what will happen to you? What will be your purpose? Money should not define you or sustain your existence. We all fall victim sometime giving money to much power and control over us. Sometime we give it so much power to the point where it becomes more alive than we are.

"The doers accept the facts, defy, and ignore them all at the same time. Yet still having to deal with the fear that the facts bring. But this fear just becomes a playground in which to challenge and change reality, despite the fear that the facts bring," (Lemon). Doubters will not ever understand the power of doer's, because their minds will not allow them too. So, they have minimum vision if no vision at all. They are mentally blind. Their mind does not have 20/20 vision; it is near sided and far sided, which explains their blurred reason of low confidence. So, getting advice from these people will only lead you toward darkness and will bring your mental high down where doubt will become your mental crown. The higher you go, the lower the volume of the doubters goes down to the point where they become deaf to your ears. The doer's are the thinkers, but the doubters are the sinkers. Never doubt yourself, but discipline yourself. If you discipline yourself you will not doubt yourself. "It's not magic to me, it's just discipline. My first time out I caught about 1,000 fish, call me the fisherman" (Lemon). It's not about who made it to the dock, but it's about who catches the most fish. It's about who can eat and stay full the most. It's not about who gets there first, it's about who stays there the longest and who has the most heart.

"Never give attention or focus to thoughts of doubt and fear, because those are moments when you can be using that time being confident," (Lemon). Never stop dreaming, because once you stop dreaming you stop thinking, and once you stop thinking you stop living. Never stop dreaming, because once you stop dreaming doubt will win and be the ultimate reason. Your mind needs your dreams to think of ways to make your fantasy into a reality. Only think about arriving at the destination and the happiness it will bring when arriving. So you can distract yourself from thinking about the travel and time that it takes to get there. Ultimately this is a way to prevent any doubt or at least drastically minimizing the doubt that you might develop along the way. You will surprise yourself and go far beyond your original goals, dreams, and expectations without even realizing it! This is when you know you are thinking BIG!

"I HAD THE GREEN LIGHT SIGNAL ALONG TIME AGO, BUT I WAS MISLED AND TRICKED INTO THINKING IT WAS RED, SO I WAS SOLITARE. BUT, NOW I SEE AND REALIZE ITS BEEN GREEN THE WHOLE TIME. SO I HIT THE GAS AND SPEEDED AWAY TOWARDS MY DREAMS."(Lemon).

SPIRIT!

(Instant Inspiration)

In order to gain instant inspiration and to change your current state of being, you must develop a different perspective and view above your negative circumstance. This is the process of instant inspiration, which will change and shift your emotional state from negative to positive: gain a new positive view about your circumstance, which will shift your focus, which will produce a more confident attitude, which will change your emotional state, which will create powerful and energetic energy, which will generate positive and optimistic thinking, which will produce a doers conversation, which will create inspiration, which will change your experience of that situation. Ultimately this process will give you back power over your spirit, now take action! Nothing can stop you, not even you, now your energy is too high and above yourself that you cannot even bring yourself down.

[MY STORY]

"The doers are hunters of success and glory," (Lemon).I am a doer! The doers do things beyond what's expected. The doers find inspiration even when it looks like termination. "If you never go treasure hunting within yourself, you will never find the gold and you will never know your true worth," (Lemon).

I was finally finished writing this book. I was relieved and accomplished. This was the most important and most precious project I have ever dedicated myself too. This book was the one thing that I can honestly say I put 100 percent of me in. This novel was my everything; it was my life work and was at the top of one of few things that I put the most effort in upon completing it. I saved all of my work on my usb drive. I was finally finished and it felt great! I grabbed an envelope, a stamp, and an extra piece of paper that I folded to put inside of the envelop, so I can hide the imprint of the usb. So no one would recognize it was an usb when I shipped it off. I have to admit I thought it was a clever move, maybe it wasn't, (laughing). But, I couldn't even tell what was in there. So, as I was walking down the street with an accomplished attitude, then I walked toward the mailbox, which I placed my mail inside with relief. The next week, my editor, which was the person I send it to, called me and told me that she received the envelop, but there was no usb inside the envelope. Also I didn't save a copy for myself, because I was going to ask my editor to send a copy to me. So she went up to the post office where this tragic event supposedly took place. They told her that the damage to the envelop does not appear that someone has stolen the device out. They said that it looks as though the usb got jammed into a machine at the post office. Also they told her that they throw away items that they cannot identity into a huge location of unidentifiable items from senders that they cannot trace the packages back too. To make a long story short I lost my life's work and to make matters worse it was thrown away into a pile as if it was garbage.

"When you accept yourself for who you are when you know you can be greater and do better, then you have failed yourself,"(Lemon). At this point my spirit was down, my attitude was negative, and my motivation was gone. However, I still had one more copy of my book that was not even as close as to being final and complete. But I picked up my motivation and I could not give up, because I came too far. I promised myself that this book will even better, more powerful, and more inspirational! I begin to write and remember certain things from my final novel and a higher level of inspiration soon arose which created a different and more powerful writing style. "I'm thankful for my misery, I'm thankful for my suffering, I'm thankful for my hell, I'm thankful for my pain. Now I see my lost just became my biggest gain," (Lemon).

[CONVERSATION THAT LEADS TO NO INFORMATION]

"The distinguishing factor that separates the realms of different worlds and realities is conversation," (Lemon). We have become so use to unbeneficial and unacceptable conversations that it has become the norm. God put us on this Earth to be social beings, because that is how we connect with each other and it is very healthy to have conversations that mean something, that can stimulate you, and can give you useful information that you can use to get to higher levels of maturity, growth, spirituality, financial gain, mental and for our mental and emotional well being. I call this type of talk that never leads to any useful information "jay talking." Basically jay talking is like a jay walking where in jay walking you are breaking the rules of consideration of vehicles while crossing the street. But jay talking is you are breaking all the rules of considering giving out useful and beneficial information. It becomes a waste of time if no one you come in contact with those who cannot help you get to another level by offering at least any one of these I mentioned above. Knowledge and information is what changes us, so if you do not have any conversations beyond what you do not know, then you will be forever in a pattern of limited beliefs and concepts, because you will not understand what you must do to get ahead in life. "Conversation that leads to no sustainable information will not lead to any influence for modification," (Lemon).

[CONSTRUCTIVE OR DESTRUCTIVE CONVERSATION]

It is a huge difference between conversations that is constructive criticism as opposed to destructive criticism. There must be a balance between constructive criticism and recognizing and valuing someone's accomplishments. Because someone can have positive motives of giving someone constructive criticism, but the results become negative and the opposite of one's motives. Ultimately this occurs, because so much constructive criticism can possibly turn into straight out criticism if not balanced out with occasional acknowledgments of strong points and achievements. People will only have a conversational approach that is within their perception of how they see, view, and expect you to be. Also to say it a similar way, people will only conversate and their conversational approach will only be at the level of what their perception of you is. So if all everyone that you surround yourself with have a negative perception of you 9 times out of 10, how positive, encouraging, and uplifting do you think your conversation will be with them? How healthy do you think it is for you to be in that environment among those who have a negative and limited perception of you? "No one will offer you healthy conversation that is beneficial to you if their perspective of you is below what you represent," (Lemon). In comparison more than likely no one will offer you positive conversation above a negative perception they have about you. You are wasting your life having conversations with people who never knew or do not know what it means to be alive. How can you grow, develop, and mature being around and wasting your time and focus with those who have negative perceptions of you? Nine times out of ten conversations among those who have a negative perception of you will be unproductive, deconstructive, and conflicting communication. Ultimately your world becomes you giving your focus and time to those who are not teaching you anything, they are not giving you any useful advice, they are not providing any words of wisdom or productive information, and they have a negative and limited perception of you that is not even close to what you represent, or how you are, or what you are working on to become. This would be expected from people that are outside of your world, but you shouldn't expect or accept these conversations among people that are inside your world. It might be time to turn your world inside out.

YOU

(Conversate above Hard Times)

"You will only be subjected to live in poverty by maintaining a view that is negatively below conscious conversation of your situation," (Lemon). Your conversation is developed through your perspective and this becomes your overall perception. Which will form your knowledge and experience of that situation and within that situation. You do not have to view anything or any situation the way that everybody does. You have the power to look at it in a different way in which will serve purposes of empowerment and inspiration to within you. Your perception will determine what level of personal experience and consciousness you will develop. That consciousness will guide your conversation. In addition your consciousness will become your level of knowledge, experiences, and attitude you will have within that situation. "If your consciousness and knowledge is not at the level or above where you want to be, then you do not have enough knowledge to get where you want to go," (Lemon). In order to gain a higher experience and to have a better attitude over your situation that is keeping you down your conversation must change and be above it. This is a formula for getting out of tough restricting realities and situations of discouragement. First gain a perspective above your situation, which will change your perception about it, then this will raise your consciousness and awareness, next it will elevate your conversation and alter your attitude, and then you will have the power to take action to get out of your situation to gain experiences beyond that situation.

"How do you expect to get out of a bad situation that would lead you towards taking action to get out that situation, if your focus is shifted in the direction of negativity and fear, which creates a terrible attitude, which generates doubtful conversation. Ultimately hindering you from having any experiences beyond your potential limiting situation," (Lemon)? If your conversation and attitude is not above the place you want to get out, then you will always be stuck in that until you change your focus of ultimately reaching a higher perception of your situation. When your perception change, you gain higher knowledge, higher consciousness, higher conversation, and then your focus will be beyond your negative circumstances that limit you from reaching your full potential. Ultimately you will gain more awareness of how to get out of that circumstance. Once you realize that you are not talking the same way as those who are in the same negative situation that you are in, and then you know your mind is above your physical circumstance. You now just have to allow your body to catch up to your mind per say. You cannot get out of something by maintaining the same perception, conversation, and think you will think of better ways to come up out that situation. Your conversation has to be above your situation. You cannot think on the same level of your situation in order to control it and make it better. "You cannot expect to get out of hard times if your conversation is not above it," (Lemon).

(HEARTLESS)

My advice is stay away from heartless people, because they have bad motives, intentions, and generate bad outcomes, situations, and circumstances. What's sad is sometimes without them even knowing themselves and realizing they themselves will become these criminals and monsters and will be harmful to society in the future. These people live within the darkness and preys upon good hearted and good intention people. These people are far from maintaining humanity and life. They are guided by corruption and viciousness, which eventually turns into devious crimes and acts. These people who are heartless are detached from positive emotions. Their spirit and soul are engraved with hatred, jealousy, bitterness, and animosity. Ultimately, our emotions and feelings are what proclaim us as human (positive or negative). Also I believe based on what emotions rule your life will determine how happy or how unhappy you will be.

Human Emotions
+
Positive Emotions

Emotion is energy in motion. Positive emotions live through joy and unity. Positive emotions are as follows: love, happiness, joy, cheer, inspiration, self-confidence, interest, curiosity, elation, certain, relief, etc. Also positive emotion is shame, guilt, and regret as well, because they set the tone for a person changing into a better intentioned person. Also they show a person who has compassion. However, these three: shame, guilt, and regret are in the category as negative emotion as too (I'll explain later within the text). The definition of love is affection, benevolence, good will, high esteem, and concern for the welfare of people. The definition of happiness is having contentment, enjoying, showing or marked by pleasure, satisfaction, felicitous and being well-adapted. The definition of joy is the emotion evoked by well-being, success, or good fortune, or by the prospect of possessing what one desires. The definition of cheer is the state of mind of feeling; mood; spirit and gladness. The definition of inspiration is the arousal of the mind to special unusual activity or creativity. The definition of self-confidence is a firm belief; trust; reliance; the fact of being or feeling certain; assurance; belief in one's own abilities. The definition of enthusiasm is inspiration as if by a divine or superhuman power; ecstasy; hence, a conceit of divine possession and revelation. The definition of curiosity is the desire to learn or know about anything; inquisitiveness. The definition of elation is a feeling or state of great joy or pride; exultant gladness; high spirits. The definition of certain is assured in mind; having no doubts; free from suspicions concerning. The definition of relief is to free from a burden: give aid or help to b: to set free from an obligation, condition, or restriction c: to ease of a burden, wrong, or oppression.

These positive emotions generate people that believe in humanity and most likely posses' positive good values such as honor, trust, respect, humility, honesty, integrity, loyalty and dignity. Which all these positive emotions lead to a healthy longer life style that blesses one with happiness, peace, and joy. Also even minimizing stress, pain, life distractions, and setbacks. Tapping into these emotions ultimately prevents and subside mental and physical diseases from surfacing or resurfacing. Also living through these emotions allows your life to be easier, less stressful and bitter. This minimizes and destroys negative emotions like, hate, jealousy, envy, greed and animosity. Adopting these positive emotions gives you a higher chance of being financially well off, because you will become more of a people person and you will love to be around people. Becoming a people person will give you an inviting spirit and aura that will allow people to be more comfortable around you and will feel they can trust you. One can gain the power of peoples trust then you can positively persuade them through utilizing positive emotions. It will be more of a chance that you will gain financial fortune. You will be more of a people person, more open minded, and not judgmental. Tapping into these positive emotions will enable you to have jobs that influence huge amounts of people such as well known comedian, doctors, inspirational speakers, actors, actresses, lawyers, professional sports players, singers, judges, preachers, CEO and presidents of companies and the president of the United States.

—

Negative Emotions

The negative emotions are as follows: anger, despair, misery, hate, rage, greed, jealousy, animosity, agony, arrogance, fear, doubtful, intimidation, guilt, shame, regret, etc. These will stop you from building great relationship and you will miss out on blessings from others you look down upon or you despise. Which one day can come where you might need these people and the ones you once looked down upon are the ones you desperately need. The definition of anger is when emotions play an organizing role in an individual experience of reality, sense of self, and orientation toward others. The definition of despair is the state of which all hope is lost or absent. The definition of misery is a state of ill-being due to affliction or misfortune. The definition of hate is dislike intensely; feel antipathy or aversion towards. The definition of rage is obsolete insanity; a furious, uncontrolled anger with great force or intense violence. The definition of greed is a selfish excessive desire to possess wealth or goods with the intention to keep it for one's self. The definition of jealousy is feelings of discontent and resentment against someone because of that person's rivalry, success, or advantage. The definition of animosity is bitter hostility or open enmity or active hatred. The definition of agony is the intense feeling of suffering from mental or physical pain. The definition of fear is a distressing emotion aroused by impending danger, and pain, whether the threat is real or imagined. The definition of doubtful is being fearful; apprehensive; suspicious; Not settled in opinion; undetermined; wavering; hesitating in belief. The definition of intimidation is to make timid or fearful; to inspire of affect with fear; to deter, as by threats; to dishearten. The definition of guilt is the state of having done a wrong or committed an offense, crime, or violation against a moral or penal law and a painful feeling of self-reproach resulting from a belief that one has done something wrong and immoral. The definition of shame is: a painful emotion caused by consciousness of guilt, shortcoming, or impropriety b: the susceptibility to such emotion. The definition of regret is pain of mind on account of something done or experienced in the past, with a wish that it had been different. Stay far away from people who display these negative emotions because they are guided by corruption and evil and will destroy anybody in their path. If you have a positive mindset and are around people who display these emotions inwardly and will eventually release it outward, they will eventually rub off on you no matter how strong minded you are. Later down the line you would catch yourself doing things that you swear up and down you would never do. I really believe the saying, "misery loves company." Misery eventually influences and destroys positive company that is of course if you allow it too.

Sometimes these people who have these emotions encoded deep within and end up doing unthinkable things like murder, rape, genocide, suicide, kidnappings, brutal beatings, assaults, etc. They typically grow up with little positive intellectual influences. Or never were influenced enough by positive emotions. They generally have been and are victims of negative emotions and were vulnerable to negative exposure that they had no control over. So, they are the victims a lot of the times before even victimizing someone else. A lot of times it is not their fault that they develop into negativity. If you know no better, you think no better, you feel no better, and you do no better. However, the true victims and are the ones that they hurt. So there is no excuse for their crimes. In the end it is always still your choice even if it was influenced by others. A lot of these people who posse's negative emotions end up with mental diseases linked to insanity. Some go mentally crazy by unfortunately creating these demons and monsters within their mind. Ultimately these demons become part of their psyche and persuade them to do ruthless acts against humanity. Historically I believe these people became like this due to never really utilizing positive emotions that should have been generated and trained from childhood. Growing up they might have been through a lot within their childhood linked to physical abuse or mental abuse. This abuse and trauma transitioned to mental trauma and disorders that lead to insanity sometimes. Also they could have had a good up bringing that was influenced by corruption of the world and they changed to negative from positive and at that point it was not their parents fault.

+-

Positive or Negative

Emotions that can be positive or negative are guilt, regret, and shame. In this text I am explaining the positive effects of these negative emotions. They are emotions from a person who still has their humanity intact. These people with these emotions still have hope and internally occupy a chance of change toward good. These people still have a pulse of conscience, which means they still maintain a little spark of positivity and changeability. These people with these emotions feel deep down inside empty/sorrow and like they did something wrong and that is the first step to change. It shows at least at one point in these peoples life they were a decent human being who was taught or developed positive emotions. However, the emotions guilt, shame and regret will allow them to develop a positive change of mind and ultimately a change of heart to positive emotions from negative emotions. If a person feels these emotions they still have a chance to change for the better, because they still feel the pain of doing something wrong and bad.

_+

Negative or Positive

However, these emotions of guilt, shame, and regret can develop into negative emotions too if contained for long extended periods of time. As well if these emotions become a repetitive memory of pain and suffering. Also, these emotions of guilt, shame, and regret can be to blame for some people's mental disease developing to cause one to be mentally unstable. These emotions eat at people's brain and mind until a brain and mind malfunction or dysfunction happens. I believe these negative emotions are what ultimately drives someone crazy and drives them to suicide. These emotions attacks you're conscious and subconscious. These emotions submit one to develop the worst of all of the negative emotions, which is hate. These emotions prevent us to move on. It prompts us to mentally stay in the past, which never allows us to heal from past hurt and trauma. These negative emotions never offer us the gift to forgive. These emotions submit us to a life of vulnerability. Ultimately, these emotions takes power from you and makes you feel like the victim. Also by feeling as the victim you have already lost. It attacks your positive train of clear thought. For example within the insert below, Nicole and Racheal, this is how these emotions can be deadly and turn from positive emotions to negative emotions of guilt, shame, and regret.

[NICOLE AND RACHAEL]

A girl named Nicole and her best friend Rachael are planning to go to a party. Nicole initially was the one who called Rachael on the phone and invited her and told her about this party at an associate's house. Rachael stayed closer to the house party then Nicole. Also, she was ready before Nicole so she called her and told her she will meet her there. So, Rachael called Nicole and told her she made it and the party is great. Nicole was on her way. Currently at the party a masked gun man forced himself or herself through the door way and began shooting and Rachael was shoot 4 times and died instantly and others was shot but just wounded. The gun man fled the scene. The police arrived and put up yellow tap signifying someone has been murdered. Now Nicole finally arrives and asks what happens and one of her peers says Rachael has been killed. Nicole goes home and drenches herself in the negative emotions of guilt, shame, regret, and sorrow. She hurtfully regrets that she invited Rachael to the party. Nicole replays this hurtful last phone call of telling her about the party. She is dreadfully sorry and drenches on sorrow. Nicole is ashamed to show up at the funeral or to speak to Rachael parents. Also she feels guilt similar to how a person on death row should feel. If she doesn't get some type of psychological help this will get worse. She will not be able to move on and she will be stuck in the past and live a life of misery. These emotions can lead to her mentally breaking down and becoming suicidal and mentally unstable to live among society.

VIEW ON EYE SIGHT, HEARING AND TOUCH

In Correlation to Positive and Negative Emotions

These three senses initially predetermine what type of man or woman a person are now and has a very high possibility of being in the future. These senses decide from a premature standpoint if people will be more of a happy positive person or a miserable negative person. Also these senses determine how mentally, emotionally, and physically healthy a person will be. "History is important, but detrimental history needs to become history and the future needs to be a new curiosity of positivity," (Lemon). Eye sight, hearing, and touch controls to which people will develop mental and physical diseases from developing a negative mindset and negative emotions that ultimately affect the body and its organs. It also can predict in theory if people will be a success, failure, or if they will be happy or miserable most of their life. These predictions are only based upon if you accept it and become it. "It is your choice to become and stay choice-less," (Lemon). Also to go as far as predict who will be our future menace to society or producers of society. These senses ultimately set the standards for what perspectives, beliefs, and values humans develop. Eye sight, hearing, and touch play huge roles regarding how people see, perceive, and view the world and what role they will play in the world. For example, if a child grows up and all he or she sees and hears is violence their more than likely to do what they saw and that will become a normal way of life. Or if a child was mentally abused and saw this growing up from parents, they are more than likely to become what they saw. Also if a child grow up being physically abused and beat they are highly susceptible to allowing themselves to be abused or becoming an abuser. However, these highly life predictions can be altered by the person that has the most power, which is "You." You ultimately determine your own fate and destiny. You have the power to rewrite your own history ahead of time. The secret to rewriting history before it happens and is history is to change your mindset, perspectives, and perceptions from negative to positive. Which will reposition and expand you to accumulate more choices and options. When you do this you will develop positive beliefs such as integrity, honor, loyalty, respect and dignity. Furthermore, these new found positive perspectives will turn into what you value and your motives will be lead by good intentions. Which naturally developing good motives and intentions will transform better decisions/choices. This will turn into good acts, and deeds. Ultimately your life will completely turn around and you will be much happier, less stressful, more financial freedom, and you will gain peace and harmony.

[BIRTH]

This is my interpretation of how it all works! I'm sure there are already other theories and proof on how this reaction occurs. However, this is my version! First a child is born, remember pure as in no personality, no identity, and practically no thoughts or sustainable ideas of focus and memory. However, through the senses of eye sight, hearing and touch these infants develop their identity. These images of visual messages, audio messages and touch messages are transferred to their minds, which develop their thoughts, ideas, feelings, reasoning, logic, understanding, rationality, behavior, memory, attitude, personality, emotions, focus, beliefs, personality, habits, deeds, behavior, attitude, energy, and actions. Ultimately through these three develops their perspectives, perceptions, experiences, and reality. In due time in the early stages of childhood these images of visual, audio, and touch messages adapt to the mind, which I stated becomes generally all their thoughts, and ultimately produces their feelings and emotions. Also these video, audio messages, and touch response develop into negative or positive emotions. Last but not the least which ever emotions they develop the most of, whether negative (hate, greed, envy, guilt, shame, jealousy, agony, despair, misery, rage, animosity, etc). Or in contrast, positive emotions like (love, happiness, joy, cheer, inspiration, etc). Ultimately which ever emotions(positive or negative) they develop stemming from what they see, hear, and feel through touch will generate their perspectives, perceptions, beliefs, values, motives, and intentions, which they will practice and live by until death or until their mindset is altered or changed for the better or for worse.

(THE GATEWAY)

Human's senses of eye sight, hearing, and touch are the gateways to our mind. Which these senses start the process of mental, emotional, and spiritual development. So whatever is processed by and in their mind transfers into feelings and what emotion (positive or negative) it will generate and turn into beliefs, perspectives, values, motives, or deeds. First it starts in the mind, and then what the mind perceives becomes a part of what a person ultimately thinks, believes, and feels. For example, parents, siblings, family, friends, associates, school, TV, media, newspapers, magazines, movies, history books and the internet all are determining factors. Most of these are responsible for these misconceptions to generate specific beliefs or stereotypes about different people, cultures, races, religions, areas, countries, and continents. Typically if one does not know from personal experience this is how one interprets, but misinterpretations most of the time come through avenues of seeing and hearing. "Become the author of your own mind. Trust me, my book has my own dialog every time," (Lemon).

THE MAIN 3 SENSES THAT ARE IN CONJUNCTION TO POSITIVE AND NEGATIVE EMOTIONS

These senses are the ability to hear (voice and audio) eye sight (see) and touch (feel) and are strongly linked to how an individual's life events possibly to a high extent might play out and which road they possibly will take given their mindset and perspectives, perceptions, circumstances, distractions and setbacks they face. But, it is ultimately up to that person to not take that route of happiness, success, or unhappiness and failure. I strongly believe these senses are in conjunction to which emotions (negative or positive emotions) one inherits from parents or produces eventually by the environment, people, psychological abuse, and physical abuse, love, and positive attention they are exposed too. Furthermore, these emotions (negative or positive) ultimately possibly predetermine what type of person you might be in the distant future. However, it is up to each individual person to rearrange their fate and destiny by changing their mindset from negative to positive.

OUTCOMES OF POSITIVE EMOTIONS DEVELOPED THROUGH THE SENSES

(Pre-maturely)

These emotions will develop within children if taught by positive thinking parents and affiliates. These kids will grow up through adolescent, teenage years, as well as adult hood with an inherited positive view and perspective on life and different cultures. These positive emotions will prohibit a life of more ups than downs, more highs than lows, more positive outcomes than negative, more financial fortunes and ultimately give them the gift of internal happiness and peace. Life will be much easier and less stressful. Relationships, friendships, and marriages will more long-term, meaningful, and more positive, than short-term. Also will have more relationship stability and security. People that posses within and incorporate more positive emotions live longer, have healthier minds, and bodies. They are healthier, because their thoughts are more positive, so that generates a healthier mind and psyche.

These kids grow up to become successful doctors, lawyers, nurses, professional athletes, preachers, teachers, police officers, judges, executives, CEO's, inspirational speakers, positive influential people, missionaries, etc. Also they more than likely become very financially successful along with being internally happy. These people grow up and get the best of both worlds. However, we all are human, so there will be bumps in the road and trying times. But, if one strays to long from a positive upbringing, one will experience more negative emotions, which will become harder and turbulent. Also negative motives, intentions, and acts will proceed. This is why it is essential for parents to install these positive views and emotions within the sensitive minds of children of today, tomorrow, and in the future. However, a child can stray and negatively wonder just as easy as an adult can. But, the good thing is when this happens, all else fells, and life is beating them up, they will remember where they came from. Which is a positive thing that they were blessed to develop more positive emotions than negative emotions through parent's guidance and discipline. Ultimately it's a higher chance that these kids when adults turn back to what they embarrassed initially childhood of positive views and emotions that produced love, peace, joy, cheer, and happiness. These positive emotions were generated through what they were exposed to as kids and these emotions originated through what they were exposed to as adolescents and teenagers. These emotions originated from what they depicted within their minds, which controlled their feelings through eye sight, hearing, and touch. Growing up their parents was more positive and encouraging than negative. Their parents or caregivers generally told them determined words such as you are bright, smart, intelligent, gorgeous, hansom, a king or a queen. They told these kids uplifting words phrases like no one can stop you and you can do anything you put your mind too. They feed these kids spirits and souls with ambition and motivation.

They heard their father telling their mother nice, romantic, and encouraging words. Such as I love you, you are wonderful and a blessing in my life, and I am thankful to have you in my life. Kids witnessed and saw the love mom and dad showed for each other. They witness love embarrassment and not love harassment. They grow up at least being exposed to positive educational and knowledgeable TV shows. Their parents exposed them to successful people and those who were thirsty for success, happiness, and prosperity. They were shown the good over the bad. Parents installed in their minds at an early age that they can have this type of car or any type of house they wanted. These children saw more smiles the frowns. They were witnesses of more good times and laughter at young ages. They acquired more positive and healthy memories than negative and disturbing memories. Mom and dad hugged and kissed them more, rather than abused them. Don't get me wrong children need lessons and discipline and respect. But it is a huge difference between disciplining a child and them understanding why they are receiving punishment. As opposed to disciplining without explanation, without making sure a child knows why this discipline is occurring, or discipline without communication. They were raised through inspiration instead of. These kids did not grow up seeing father physically abusing mother. Nor did they hear or could remember father and mother verbally and mentally abusing each other on a day to day basis. These children were patted on the back, told great job, and awarded for their accomplishments.

It's most likely these kids became productive positive citizens of society with good motives and intentions. They became successful teachers, preachers, doctors, lawyers, presidents, scientists, senators, geniuses, governors, executives, and astronauts. Also others became successful NBA, MLB, NHL players and principals. They became the people with the most sanity, happiness, intelligence, and fortune. They as growing up had less distractions and setbacks. They were fortunately mentally protected from a lot of things that would have caused them in the future to develop varies psychological issues. I realized it's a great thing to protect your kids from what will cause great mental disturbance. However, I realized the same thing that you protect your children from is the same thing they need to know, realize, and understand before being exposed to it. The same thing you try to protect them sometimes from is the same thing that strips them from security and devours and eats them alive. I think kids need to get exposed by parents to the same thing that they are trying to protect them from. However, it's a way to do everything. Positive exposure is the answer. Kids must be told the truth, so they will not grow up lost and develop very high levels of fear, anxiety, paranoia, and panic. What I believe is that the world will eat them alive if parents don't positively teach kids how to prepare for appetizers, dinner, and dessert!

The ultimate reason of their success is given to a positive upbringing than negative. Which they were blessed with clearer thinking, less distraction, setbacks, and less mental inflicted trauma. They more than likely develop positive healthy perspectives and perceptions. Inevitably these kids saw and heard majority only things that maintained the normal healthy balance of their mental makeup. Which eventually generated more positive emotions, which supported which believes and values they followed. Furthermore, theses beliefs and values influenced better and more positive motives, intentions, and acts. They ultimately generated the power of clear thinking.

OUTCOMES OF NEGATIVE EMOTIONS DEVELOPED THROUGH THE SENSES

(Pre-maturely)

These children who grow up to become adults have minimal chances of being a productive mentally healthy thinking person. A lot of them become victims of mental, psychological, and physical abuse. A lot of times they become victims before they become the perpetrator and predators. Which by the way if they get this lucky to life through all the mental and psychological trauma even before they become the perpetrator. These kids have higher possibilities to become future killers, drug addicts, murderers, robbers, terrorists, suicide victims, etc. They are most likely to become menaces of society. However, to me that society that they are a menace to is the same society that only gave them that option to be what they was expected to be. You only become what you can truly see and what you see from within is what you become!

A lot of these kids become victims of society or accomplishes to murder. Because, they become all they know through generally how they were raised. They were raised and we all are raised through very important senses such as eye sight, hearing, and touch. Growing up from infant-hood, childhood, teenage hood, and then adulthood more than normal for them is all they see is frowns. All they see is no one smiling for something that is of good intent and cheer. They witness father not catering to mother nor showing her any type of love and appreciation. Neither do they see mother embracing father with appreciation or respect. They fall victim to love, peace, fortune, and happiness. This explains why their sanity is always in a balance.

These children grow up and don't hear I love you and they don't hear you are God's gift to me. Also they don't hear father and mother saying they love each other. They don't hear mother and father telling them they are beautiful, handsome, smart, intelligent, and wonderful. They don't hear son or daughter you can be anything you put your mind too. They on the other hand hear you are stupid, slow, use common sense, dumb, and will be nothing. This is verbal abuse, which becomes mental and emotional traumatizing. Later on it generates into how they see themselves, how they think and feel about themselves. Ultimately they take their hurt out on innocent by standers or immediate family members, cousins, and friends. Then they bring this attitude where every they go. Which this attitude is hurting them the most. They are victims of false hope if any hope at all. In my opinion it is as if they are prisoners of war without even physically being captured. Which they are MPOW (mental prisoners of war). I say this, because mentally they are suffering and that is much more worse, then physical pain. This becomes all they know is mental suffrage, which develops their negative mindset. Ultimately generating negative emotions and feelings of misery, turmoil, rage, jealousy, and animosity. They develop detrimental and inhibiting perspectives and perceptions.

These kids grow up being physically abused. They most likely are getting raised by parents who discipline them in anger and rage. So this is not justified discipline. Because a lot of times these parents punish these kids while per-occupied with outside variables that negatively effects the judgments and decisions for discipline for these children. A lot of times this discipline is not discipline based off what the child has done, but rather then what they are being subjected to in world affiliations and complications. This turns into years of physical abuse, which later turns into mental and emotional trauma. Which curses them with sometimes a lifetime of panic, fear, anxiety, paranoia, trust issues, and confusion. They are more susceptible to becoming products of their environment. Which in fact they have become a product of their environment in relation to being a product of their home.

[POSITIVE CORE VALUES OF EXPECTANCY]

People who are more positive than negative have more a mindset of values such as honor, respect, dignity, loyalty, trust, honesty, and integrity. The definition of honor is a token of esteem paid to worth; a mark of respect; or a ceremonial sign of consideration. The definition of respect is to consider or treat with deference or dutiful in regard, or to avoid violation or interference. The definition of dignity is bearing conduct, or speech indicative of self respect or appreciation of an occasion or situation. The definition of loyalty is the state or quality of being loyal; faithfulness to commitments or obligations. In other words this means being a man or woman of your word and sticking to what you say through your action. The definition of integrity is adherence to moral codes and ethical principals; soundness or moral character; and an unbroken undiminished condition. These peoples positive mindset leads the way for positive emotions, motives, intentions, actions, and deeds. These people are more human than inhuman. They live by these set of rules of life. These people will produce the positive side effects of guilt, shame, and regret. These emotions when referred to positively are all signs of people with good moral and values. Which shows that they feel bad, have a conscious and a good heart and realizes they did something wrong against another human being. Also these emotions describe a person who will change for the better sooner than later. These people are more trust worthy and more honest. Also, these people with these values tend to be more peaceful and don't cause chaos or misfortune for others. However, people do change over time so you must always be aware. We are all human and sometime we all have are ups, down, and gloomy days, and do things we regret. These people I call positive value thinkers make life easier and society safer. They will be more encouraging then discouraging. They are more supportive than non supportive. You need to become a positive value thinker so life will be easier, less complicated, and you will be more successful and happier. They say never judge a book by its cover, which I am an advocate of this slogan. Never stereotype, but you still must be wise and aware in regards to those who lurk and prey upon you.

[NEGATIVE CORE VALUES OF EXPECTANCY]

People with these negative core values are just the opposite of people of core positive values. Their character displays dishonesty, unloyal, disrespect; they have no dignity or integrity. They do not follow the laws of respect and positive order. Ultimately without law and order we will have a country of pure chaos and anarchy. God supports order and laws, but righteous order is what God advocates. Negative core value people are more likely to be backstabbers and liars. They are more likely to set you up. They only live for power, control, and money. These people are all over, it doesn't matter what town or area. They produce emotions such as hatred, jealousy, and animosity. No one is perfect, so everyone has experienced at least one of these emotions. However, the negative value thinkers allow these emotions to lead their life and actions. You must use your new found ability of mental awareness to spot these people. They will kill and murder sometimes just to prove a point. Also will kill just to kill without cause. Negative value thinkers will make your life miserable, because they have no hope or faith. Hope and faith is positive and it comes from God! Remember if someone always talk negatively, unproductively, and never has anything good to say, what type of person does that truly make them? What emotions lead their life? What believes and values do they really stand for? "What ever someone's motives are will always trace back to what they believe in," (Lemon). What are their true motives and intentions? Ultimately what actions will they act out against you or the ones you love? Furthermore, by considering all these variables you probably have prevented your own murder and others around you more times then you noticed. However, the only reason you didn't notice and others didn't notice is because, you are still alive and they are s well. It's weird how when someone dies tragically or gets murdered, how examiners and corners can in detail show and explain how this person died. But, we don't have experts that show up on the scene to teach people how to stay alive and how not to end up like this corpse.

5TH PHASE

Develop Mental Awareness
(Character Counts)

Mental awareness a high level of a survival instinct ability that can and will in certain circumstances prevent and save your life or others around you. It is an enhanced ability of great predictability and understanding of how things truly are, people, and situations really are. It gives you the power to view the big picture and truth about things, situations, and people. Mental awareness gives you the power to see through people's character, which in turn gives you a higher sense of their motives and intentions. This ability can and will save your life by preventing your murder as well as those you love. Also it means to distinguish which people are posing as the predator and see you as the prey. It is a mental ability to take in consideration all aspects of people's character. Which will allow you to be more accurately predict what is now and in the future their motives, intentions, whether constructively positive or destructively negative. Also mental awareness can be utilized within the work environment. Furthermore, on a good note this ability can rebuild your credibility among co-workers, and management at the workplace. Which ultimately can and will prohibit rapid movement up the success ladder within the company. Also mental awareness can help Management manage more effective in a positively productive way. Mental awareness is the art of higher survival instincts through examination of everything and everybody around you, and realizing when someone or people are insulting you, disrespecting you and not taking you serious. Mental awareness you can use at work to get a better position and title, which will allow you to make a lot more money, gain more respect, creditability, and responsibility. Ultimately mental awareness will give you leverage and gain respect and trust, which will indeed present you more much more financial opportunities and fortune. Also, mental awareness can be used outside of work, particularly on a street level. I will discuss this part of mental awareness further in the chapter.

However, the other the first part of mental awareness I will discuss now is related to gaining an account of how someone or people will impact your life as in a positive or negative way. It is a way to distinguish what beliefs and values someone has, which will give you a better recollection and account of what their motives, intentions, and actions will highly possibly become toward you. Mental awareness is a preventative method of enhanced mental abilities of reading people to develop a vivid analysis of what to expect of them presently, in the near, and far future. It will minimize the risk and maximize the possibilities of better decision of the risk to play out in your favor, interests, as well as others. MA is great precision and a great account of someone's character. Which, will give you leverage in relation to high possibility of their motives, intentions, and actions as I said prior. Ultimately by realizing this you can precisely predict which emotions and feelings (either negative or positive) will be directed toward you. Mental awareness can be used on a work level and a street level. Also overall it will allow you to realize if your image is negative or positive. As well as if people's mindsets are negative or positive about you at work or outside of work.

Ultimately having a negative mindset portrays negative values and beliefs. Furthermore, displaying negative emotions will only show up in action. Mental awareness will give you higher predictability skills of what to expect of people presently and in the future. Which by having greater predictability skills will give you insight on what someone motives and intentions highly might possibly be, which will save your life and others you love. In other words people will have a positive impact on your life or negative. Ultimately when going places, choosing friends, companions, and marriage partners mental awareness will put you more in control of your life, happiness, financial future and your future in general.

DEVELOPING WORK SMARTS (BENEFITS OF MENTAL AWARENESS AT WORK)

Trust is a Must!

Mental awareness is a measure of being observant and determining when people are insulting you, disrespecting you and not taking you serious. Once you realize this you can change the negative perspective and image management has about you. Which, by changing their perspective of you to positive will ultimately give them the trust and confidence in you. This transformation will allow you to gain more creditability, respect, and responsibility, which will enable you to move up rapidly in that company. Everything takes time, so do not get discouraged. Eventually you will see a gradual upward flow of respect and trust. When you gain trust and respect you gain a higher pay check! Trust equals money rush! Trust equals financial freedom! Trust is not gained automatic it is gained manual. "Receiving trust you must get out of the car and sincerely wash and cater to it," (Lemon). Gaining trust is mental work and sweat. But, once you gain it that's less physical work and sweat, which offers your body a rest. Also you will be offered higher and more company respectable positions. If you are not offered these positions, don't be discouraged, because now you have the leverage of respect and trust to acquire about these positions of interest. They will listen and take in consideration all aspects of your new found credibility, respectability, and accountability.

INSULT HD

(High Definition)

Mental awareness is realizing when someone or people are insulting you, disrespecting you and not taking you serious. This strategy is most prevalent at work, which will show you how you need to change your position, behavior, attitude, and conversation. My theory on how to detect and realize when you personally are getting this treatment by management is to be very observant how they approach and respond to you. Also watch how they approach and respond to others and compare and contrast. Generally remember the work place is supposed to be considered a place of professionalism. Which management are the ones who represent the company and should be the ones who respect and uphold this code to the highest extent. Watch how a supervisor or manager approach and respond to you. If they are always unprofessional with you and are always joking more than being professional with you and serious, they most likely don't take you serious. Look at it like this if they are 85% more likely to be unprofessional and not serious approaching and responding to you, then the other 15% they are professional and serious with you, obvious they do not respect you or take you serious. Once you gained this data, the strategy is to change your position, attitude, and limit conversation. Conversation should only be about work related situations and never about anything beyond the work place. So, your chances at this company of moving up the success ladder is very slim. If management does not respect you, this is already a bad sign of a bad work relationship that is between you and them. No one will consider anyone a promotion if they do not have the respect and confidence of those who are in higher positions where you one day want to be.

Then, be more observant and look around and consider how management approaches and responds to other workers and staff. Then, after a while if you see a huge difference of respect, acknowledgment, and professionalism. Now you will have a clue as to what your destiny and fate was within that company. If someone never takes you serious, there is no way they can respect you. They probably talk about you behind your back, because they think you are a joke and you don't even know it. But, if you use this strategy of mental awareness you will now know what is the company perception of you is. However, now you can alter and change your destiny and fate of being unsuccessful within that company. This negative mindset from management will stunt your growth within that company and they will never offer you a position of leadership. Furthermore, you will not make the type of money as you would if you were taking serious and respected. As you can see respect is very vital to financial success and fortune. Without respect on any level of living among people you have nothing. So, to a point you need to consider what people around you and those you come in contact on a daily basis think of you. But, of course don't live your life according to what people think and say about you, but in certain cases it's important, such as the work environment in order to be considered for higher positions.

[WORKER ACKNOWLEDGMENT]

This is another way how you can change the negative perspective of you and gain the professionalism, respect and seriousness from management. Always stick to the code of professionalism and seriousness. When a manager approaches you unprofessional, counter them with professionalism. When management approaches and responds to you through unrelated conversation that is not work related and tries to make the conversation personal, counter it with seriousness and keep your conversation within the boundaries of work. Furthermore, do not add on and become an advocate of a personal conversation when making this life changing transformation. Of course do not offend those who have the power to put you in higher positions of more opportunity. So, I am not saying ignore management, but just unconfrontationally let them know you want to keep your conversations within the limits of work. Maintain professionalism and seriousness every time they approach and respond to you. This is how you really will realize what their view of you is. Obviously they don't take you serious or respect you if they continuously approach and respond to you in an unprofessional and in a never serious way while in a professional and serious environment.

Take this approach for however long it takes for them to change their negative perspective about you to a positive respectable one. This strategy will allow your respect level to go up and you will move up the success ladder within that company. They will start to treat you different and become more professional and serious with dealing with you. Ultimately you will gain the respect and trust of this company. This will transition to management asking approaching you with more responsibility. This responsibility will eventually come in the form of supervisor, manager, general manager, district manager, and ultimately even CEO and President. If you don't acquire these successes you probably should consider working for a different company. Ultimately it was not your fault, some people just don't want to give others higher opportunity, because they feel threatened. If you look at it like that you are becoming the person you should be, not because you are a threat to someone. But, because they see you as competition now. You are a winner either way it goes!!!

[WORKERS]

Discredited Conversation
(Company Demoralization)

This is a continuation of your transformation to respect and higher position. Professionalism means when at work any and all conversation should be related to work. So any conversation that is not work related should be considered unprofessional. Furthermore any conversation that does not relate to the operation of the business is not work related and you should consider personal, which it is your choice to talk about it. Which I encourage and urge you not to talk about anything personal or not work related. At least just for the time you are trying to gain trust, respect, and credibility. This conversation somehow gives others leverage over you, which allows them to negatively label and judge you based upon your personal life. Anything that is personal is your business and nobody even management does have a right to access that part of your life. I know people joke around and get personal to have a little fun at work to make work more worth working, comfortable, and less stressful. However, allowing work to get to personal allows people to get to comfortable with you and slowly but might open a door to try you and indirectly or directly disrespect you. This causes them to begin to be very unprofessional and not take you serious. Which the level of respect has drastically gone down or even worse if they never respected you from the beginning, consider yourself on the negative end of respect. Have you ever wondered why in ten years you have not been offered a new position or promotion? You have no respect or trust! Sometimes joking too much and playing can submit you to a label of not taken serious and that leads to disrespect. Also it leads to management not taking you serious or viewing as unprofessional. Ultimately you will become a big joke and will stop you from moving up in the company. This label will deny you the chance of higher position opportunities, because management will not take you serious and think you are irresponsible and irrelevant.

[DISRESPECT BELOW ZERO]

It's unfortunate, because some people don't even know that they are being disrespected, being insulted, and not taken serious due to higher education, communication, intelligence, and understanding in various positions of company business practices. I call this disrespect below zero (cold hearted respect). This people have no respect or care for the people who are responsible for their sometime overestimated bank accounts and shopping sprees. Trust me I am not taking any credit or hard work from the ones who made it, did it, and got the top. I'm not taking any discipline or determination from them, but some people forget where they came from. I believe the same place that made you can destroy you, so it is in your best interest to consider that. These people tend to have a higher vocabulary level then others who did not seek out the same education or didn't have to money to gain such a privilege. So, sometimes lower education, minimum understanding people cannot filter and figure out different language and other means of higher communication and intelligence. So, in retrospect they just stay in their little hole of confusion and intimidation and say nothing. Ultimately these are the ones who do not move up in a company and remain idol and financially stationary. Also these are the people who don't know or realize when they are getting insulted, disrespected or not taken serious due to the lack of terminology of communication they know.

[BUSINESS PROFESSIONALISM]

Management

Typically the workplace environment is proclaimed and supposes to be a place of professionalism. This means workers and management suppose to respect and uphold a law of special conduct supported by the law of human ethics of treatment of decency, fairness and respect. My definition of having professionalism is using the words that you know and expressing them in a very confident way of sounding out all words, completing thoughts, ideas and sentences. Also, being assertive, humble, speaking in a tone of grace, but at the same time with clarity and power. Professionalism does not always have to do with using big giant words of terminology. It means treating everyone with respect no matter what type of business it is, whether a warehouse or office building. Also treating everyone the same no matter what color, culture, religion or mental intellectual level one is presently on. This is how you keep your business comfortable and maintain reliable productive enthusiastic workers. This is how to manage a large group of people with different personalities. A group of people with varies personalities will present a chaos of miscommunication if these personalities are not approached positively. What you do not want is a work environment that much of the day is consumed with miscommunication. Because, you'll have a day full of more miscommunication than the work not getting done. You never want workers working in high irritation and frustration. Because, it will show in the production of their work attitude and production altitude. If you take this positive approach you will receive more positive responses. Which the work environment will have peaceful energy.

Which that energy will flow within the minds and bodies of the workers. Which their actions will not produce massive hesitation. Ultimately the workers will work with grace and positivity, which will enable them to concentrate much more. Ultimately this focus will limit high levels of panic and overwhelming stress. Fortunately for the company these limited lowered amounts of panic and stress will limit mistakes and misjudgments. Furthermore, company time will be spent figuring out ways to accommodate customers rather than concentrating time on figuring out ways of minimizing company workers mistakes. This will present the company with record sells just off the basis of a different approach to its workers, which will generate a better response. Also, workers will not have a problem helping out and even will volunteer to assist others, which will take stress off of supervisors and managers. Also work will be done at a much quicker estimation. Furthermore, this extra time workers are saving the company just off of being generous will save company millions of dollars yearly. Ultimately the company's production will be produced with much better precision and care from employees. This will offer company growth and financial stability and become a very profitable fortune company.

[STREET SMARTS]

Developing Street Smarts
(Mental Awareness utilized on a Street Level)

Mental awareness can be used within a street environmental level as well, but with a twist. As said before mental awareness is being observant and realizing when someone or people are insulting you, disrespecting you and not taking you serious. This is a positive defense mechanism of survival. In the streets this strategy will ensure a safer and longer life for you and those you love. Being observant in the streets will give you the upper hand, because to survive in the streets means you must adapt to the environment, the people in it, and around it. You must think ahead past those who plot against you and want to bring death and pain toward you. Using mental awareness on a street level can and will stop and prevent you from getting robbed, assaulted and even stop your own murder from happening. Also it can and will prevent others from being a victim of your acquaintances, associates and risky where abouts. You can save your life and redirect your destiny and fate from unhonrable to honorable with a blink of a different mindset.

Ways to realize when someone or people are insulting you, disrespecting you and not taking serious on a street level are very essential ways of survival and adding to your life expectancy. Which I might add is a very dangerous situation when you do not have street respect. Which I need to add, I do not mean street respect in regards to drugs, cars, clothes, money, and women. I mean just the opposite, gaining and demanding respect so people won't or think twice about killing you over drugs, money, cars, clothes and women. That right there is what you want; you want them to think twice. Thinking twice is hesitation and that is good in the streets. If that second thought isn't there, then they are too confident in a negative way. Just as I said within text about developing work smarts it is very essential to demand and gain respect. It is very necessary on a street level as well. The big difference is at work it is essential for position and financial elevation, but on the streets it is essential for life and survival elongation.

Ways to realize when someone or people are disrespecting you, insulting you, and not taking you serious on a street level are very essential ways of survival and adding on to your life expectancy. Which I will add is a very dangerous situation when you do not have street respect while being on a street level.

The ones who insult you, disrespect you, and don't take you serious are the ones who need an audience, crowd, and other people around to look and appear big and intimidating. However, they are the ones really are intimidated, because they this is what they do to feel good about themselves. This is what they do to build their self esteem and confidence up. So in reality these are the ones who are insecure, vulnerable, and they are prey and don't realize it. So this is another reason why you need not to be intimidated by these fake so-called predators. They are the ones who need a lot of TLC (tender loving care), laughing. Be aware of these people because, they are backstabbers, deceivers, manipulators, jealous ones, and liars. Ultimately you cannot and should not trust these ones. They are the ones who will set you up. They are the crowd pleasers, so in actuality they are the followers.

These people, who don't respect you, voluntarily directly insult you on purpose, and don't take you serious see you as weak and see you as the prey. They view you as an easy predictable target of high possible success. When the enemy knows you are predictable and have fear in your heart, they have already won the battle and war! You are defeated without even retreated or surrendering. You lost without even fighting!

TKO

(Termination known obvious)

They know what your next step is even before you take it, so they will always be a step ahead. This is very dangerous. This is a possibility of why there are so much robbery, murders, rapes, and kidnappings. My motto is the more unpredictable you are in this negative world and on a street level, the safer and better you are from perpetrators and predators. For a general predator, they like easy prey and easy prey is predictable prey. It's too much of a risk to chase plot against someone who is unpredictable, because they will not ever know what to expect and that will build to much uncertainty and some doubt in them. Positive Doubt is good in the streets, when protecting yourself from being a victim. Positive doubt is when a predator has second thoughts and produces doubt, which stops and prevents an attacker from plotting, because they develop uncertainty and prevents one from being a future victim. Never give anyone any reason to develop negative confidence (as I call it) in regards to you. Negative confidence is when people gain confidence from the point of view of viewing you as an easy target or easy victim without any doubt in their mind. If a predator has high levels of positive doubt, then eventually the so called predator will feel threaten by you and that will drastically minimize the chances of you ever becoming a victim or prey. These predators lack true positive core values of respect, trust, honesty, loyalty, dignity and integrity. Without these values there will not be true positive order, there will be complete confusion and chaos. Today's youth just need to be retaught these values which would stop a lot of the violence. I must say sometime when it's your time to go it's your time to go, but you to a point control when and where it's your time to go. So stop being so predictable and calculated to people who are plotting against you.

Also, everyone follows, but make sure that you know what you are following and that your leader has some type of respectable and trust worthy principals they live by. Which this type of leader will look out for the best interest of his or her followers. When you die and rest in peace, make sure you left peace on earth before you died, not wrath and pain. It doesn't matter, I will still leave my legacy, even if it has to be left through the eyes and memories of my enemy. Which those memories will not even give my enemies any satisfaction and will force them in thought to respect me.

[GOOD IS THE ILLUSION]

Let me explain this title good is the illusion. We need to tell the truth and reveal the truth about the world and people. Good is the illusion of course when you do not know the other side of what's not said to be good. When you know the other side of what's not good, then you have the truth and you are prepared for what real. The truth is the world is not all good and positive. Everything is not good and everybody doesn't have good intentions. However, do not categorize everyone in the same category. But, if you think everything and everybody is good and looks out for you and your safely, then you are in trouble, because they are not. The teachings of good is great, but what you do not get taught most of the time you will fall victim too. I am not advocating teaching what is known as bad, but one must know what he or she are up against and must know the operations of that which is its opposite. Basically there is always an opposite of everything, for example good/bad, right/wrong. Up/down, positive/negative, yes/no. So, if you are just taught one side of something, then you will be naive to the opposite. You will always get attacked and become a victim of what you were never taught to pay attention too. Listen, I am not advocating or encouraging the teachings of so-called evil and wickedness. But however, I am advocating to make sure you have an understanding of what is the opposite of what you are not and what you do not believe in. Find out why to anything that is the opposite of what you believe or follow. Because the same thing that you do not believe in is the same thing that you fight against. So, how can you protect yourself, put up a good fight, and defeat something that you never were prepared to battle against? How could you put up an equal fight against something that you do not understand? You will lose every time with a one track mind of being naive to what's perceived as evil and bad.

The real truth is that the world is not good and positive. This is how it is portrayed and how most teach their children growing up, which is good principals, morals, ethics, and values. Which this is great for the development of a good person and a healthy thinking person. However, the opposite that which will make them sick will only achieve this through neiveness and a lack of knowledge. They teach them these principals to protect kids from becoming the opposite of what they do not want them to be. But if they do not know the other side of what they are not, then they can easily fall victim to that reality that they do not know about. However, the reality is that good is not the leading founder of this world, nor does it has the most influence over someone. What I mean when I say good is the illusion is the perception that the world is all good. If you see it like this then people will always lead you to danger and situations that will lead you to an early grave or early prison sentence. Good is the illusion, because you will always find the truth within the deep lies and the darkness. The ones who do not know what is within the darkness will always think they have the truth by playing it safe and being comfortable staying in the light. But what good is it to be in the light, but not know if you are in a light of truth? So are you really in the light if you do not have a truer and deeper knowledge of what you are in and of what is on the outside of what you are in. The same thing that is on the outside of what you are in is the same thing that can see you, but you cannot see it. Basically make sure you know what is on both sides of a situation. Just to put things in perspective, the idea of good is superficial and is a mask over what is the true reality of the world. Good is a false illusion that distracts you from the truth and reality that the world is not good at all. I support and advocate a choice to be good and positive. I am not saying don't be good, all I am saying is know what is not good. In many cases you will always find more truth in what is called negativity, because that is where you will find the most honesty. The power in knowing both sides of a story is that you will always know why something is and will be prepared for any ending and will have the power to make your own as well.

[A SMILE COULD BE A DEATH SENTENCE]

Be careful who you smile around because a smile is welcoming and inviting. You do not want to welcome or indirectly encourage those who think you are weak and easy prey. A smile could be deadly and an invitation to be payed attention to in a negative way. What you want is less or no attention toward you. You do not want to welcome death. You want to make death think twice before or not even gain enough confidence to pursue your life. In the streets what you want is people assuming to believe that they cannot trust you. This is what you want, people not knowing if they can trust you. You want and need respect! Because the more someone trusts you the more they think they know you. So you want and need more respect and make sure those who ever thought to cross you do not trust you. Because if they don't trust you, then they do not know what to expect from you and that will develop doubt and uncertainty within them. Which that low confidence will highly stop and prevent any actions of negative intent or motive toward you. Do not cling to large crowds. You are not hiding, but you are just being cautious and smart about people you are around. Don't stay too long around people, because you do not want to build too many personal relationships that they would think they know you. Ultimately you are safer and will be the most powerful the less anybody know you or think they know you. Unless they think they know they cannot cross you. People who think and believe they know you will be more likely to disrespect you or set you up as before someone who didn't trust you or think they know you. In the streets you are the safest and have the most power, when most people don't know you, don't believe they know you, but still respect you. The less information people know about you, the better you are. What you want is for predators to be up in the air and a bit confused when it comes to you. You do not want so many people to have their mind made up about who you are, what you are capable of, nor what you are not capable of. The less communication the better you are. Do not talk about anything personal or important information that would make someone think you guys are friends or cool. A lot of times your so-called friends are the ones who will back stab you. I believe you probably are much safer around your enemies, because you can trust them much more then friends, because at least you know their intentions and motives. Which you do not know your friends and they could have hidden agendas, but you do not know because your guards are always down with them. All I am saying is you need to be aware of who you are around and you do not want to smile, welcome, and invite death to your life. In all cases it is ultimately the mentality of those you are around and not necessarily all the time the area. I am not saying do not smile at all; please do not take this passage beyond what it is intended to be. I am just saying you have to know your surroundings and who is surrounding you. No one should be able to control when and where you smile, but you should know who you are smiling around and who you are inviting in your life.

TRANSFORMING FROM PREY TO BECOMING THE PREDATOR

When being the predator you still can maintain the right motives and good intentions. A great strategy is to initially keep your guards down, so then it will be a lot easier to see people for who they really are. Sometimes appear kind of weak and vulnerable, so you will be able to see the people who will try to take advantage of you appearing to be weak. Don't quickly speak, react or attack, because you do not know who is who yet. You don't know who are your friends, allies or who is a self proclaimed predator (in their mind for now momentarily). Now you will see who will intentionally and voluntarily disrespect you. But, sometimes people disrespect others unintentionally or involuntarily and do not realize it, but you still must in an unconfrontational, non-threating, and non-violent way let them know they are doing this, so you do not by mistake label them as a predator. You must give this attention to this matter by simply unconfrontationally taking that person to the side and making them aware that you do not uphold to their conduct. If they continue to do these acts after warning them, then you know what category to place them in and I'm sure it won't be best pal of the year.

(TRANSFORMING)

However, sometimes we get into relationships, easily befriend and trust people, or easily fall for the trap of people that is out to hurt and violently harm us. I am not saying don't trust anyone, but be very careful when giving out something so precious, priceless, and profound. The people you give your trust to without knowing if you can truly trust them, are the ones who will plot against you and bring danger and harm your way. A lot of times you can never truly know if you can trust someone, but that is where your mental awareness instinct kicks in. This will maximize the percentage of making the right choice when choosing those to trust. The people who take your trust for granted are the predators. The predators are the ones you befriend with the motive of crossing you. They are the ones that voluntarily set out to hurt and harm people they see as prey. You must become a master strategist and detailer before the fact, leading up to the fact and after the fact. You must become the best at counter attacks, submissions, retreats, and surrenders. This is why we must gain the ability to distinguish who has good intentions and who has bad intentions. You must gain the ability as to who has negative interior motives and unrighteous intentions. Mental Awareness teaches you how to stay alive longer and it's a training guide to living amongst bad intentioned people with corrupted beliefs. "You do not want to be a by-product of anybody's destructible belief system that is in conflict with your righteous motives and intentions," (Lemon).

A strategy is to allow your guards to be down and appear a bit weak and you will recognize those who are out to harm you, because those will be the ones who verbally (through ways of embarrassment and excessively aggressively voluntarily trying to intimidate and challenge you), emotionally and physically try to abuse you. These are way to easily zero down and realize the people who think they are the predator and you are the prey. They see you as weak, vulnerable, easily surrendering, and not putting up much of a fight. Now you have let your guards down and you see those who took advantage of you appearing weak, naive, misinformed, and vulnerable. Now you see the ones you go out their way to make you look bad and think hard to put you to public shame in and mockery. These are the ones who verbally will try to intimidate and see how you respond to their threats. Now you realize the ones who are not friends or allies. These people are the predators. "My mother taught me how to stay on the straight and narrow. But I figured out I had to still learn how to shot a bow and arrow," (Lemon).

[PREY NOW PREDATOR]

The first step into transforming from the prey into the predator is changing your mindset. If you think you are the prey, you will feel like the prey, which in fact you will become it. This is the time to implement your strategy
, think as they think, but far beyond what they think you will think, which they already set their mind and think they are the predator and you the prey just off their arrogance alone in many cases. The way you realize how they think and to gain leverage is to realize their understanding.

"No one can plan in the direction or take any action above what they do not understand or what their arrogance will not give them vision to see,"(Lemon). When you realize their understanding you can highly predict their moves and actions. In addition once you realize what they know and if they do not have a higher understanding then you, then that tells you that you are more of a threat to them then they are to you, but they do not know this. Now you realize that you will have a much more advanced, so farfetched, and knowledgeable plan then they would ever think to think. This is the time to think beyond them for great surprise attacks, counter attacks, and diversions. But, retreats, surrender, and defeat on their part. Never let them know you know they think they are the predator. Because if you tell them you know they think they are the predator then, they will be more aware and have time to plot and restratigize, which will indeed put you more susceptible to becoming the prey. The only difference is now you are expected prey. What you want to be is unexpected prey, which is the same thing as now you being the predator. Adapt to how they think, then, think the opposite of what they think (this makes you the predator).

Next, revise and calculate an irrational and unusual plan that they will not suspect, which will enable victory for sure. Think about it, you now know they think they are the predator and see you as the prey, but they don't of course not know you know they think they are the predator and you the prey. So, who is really secretly now the predator and who is unaware they are now the predictable prey?

I say this to say you now know their motives and intentions, so you have the upper hand now. You are the predator now, without them even knowing or it, but soon enough they will. You are in control, because now they are predictable, usual, practical, and their steps are now easily calculated, because you know and have a very accurate account of what their plans and plots are or have a very high expectancy of what it will be. Now you can sit back and think past their obvious boring plan and surprise them with something they never would think you being the prey would foster up. One of the ultimate strategies of transforming from the prey to the predator is to not break under pressure. Because when you do, you lose focus. You can now surprise them with something unthinkable on your part, because now you know and have a vivid account of what they are thinking and their plan. A persons plan will not go beyond the limited knowledge that they know. Which, you now have the power to think past their now obvious and apparent plan. You now have the power of time being by your side. Now you can think and master a plan they would never expect or think to think about or think to think you would think about. I call it the Unthinkable plan! "You can't even think past my last thoughts. So what makes you think that you can bring me the same thing that I brought you, especially considering the last time we fought," (Lemon).

A lot of predators are arrogant and that is what turns them into the prey. To the so called predator your surprise will be unpredictable, uncalculated, unorthodox, original, unsuspected and unscheduled to them. They more than likely will not be prepared for it especially if they are as I said before arrogant. This will insure either retreat, surrender, defeat or a victory! A predator more than likely don't have a vision past a vision because they are too arrogant and closed minded to envision their downfall. So I say again who is now the predator and who is really the prey? I have a saying, "It's funny how they think they are the predator, but I just laugh it off, because I'm ten steps ahead of you. So, who is really the predator and remind me again why I should be scared of you. So, I see your plan and plot, now I can rethink which means now I control the time on the clock, the tick and the tock," (Lemon). People give other people the power to be the predator. A lot of times people don't know when they are being preyed upon, so they don't have a choice other than being the prey at that time of preditation.

However, now you have the insight of reversing from being the prey to the predator. Ultimately you have the power of realizing the signs of a predator and not becoming the prey. Also on a more positive note, don't turn into the predator for means of vengeance or retaliation. But, the best policy is simply walking away from the association, affiliation and congregation of these people with reason of knowing their present, near future and far future motives and intentions. But, don't be scared of people and never give people power to scare, put fear in your hearts and intimidate you. If you do in your mind and heart you are creating and giving them the power of a predator, which will only make it easier for them to prey upon you just off of your fear alone. "Sometimes you must fight fire with fire. However, not with the intention to burn. But with the motive to make sure those who burnt you never think to try to light another match again," (Lemon).

[ABSTAIN FROM VIOLENCE]

I just want to reassure readers that I am not teaching practices of violence and retaliation methods. I am simply giving insight on strategies of better and smarter ways of not becoming the violentee or the victim of a hanis murderous crime. "Evil is deceptive through unpredictability, but good is predictable through continuous patterns of order and honesty," (Lemon). The solution for good people is to be as unpredictable as evil, but with the intentions to bring peace. This chapter transforming from the prey to the predator is a way to give insight on how to spot people with predatory mindsets. This chapter shows how to recognize wolves that prey upon sheep. Also a means to provide a way for more accurate predictability skills when it comes to the people they choose to be around and places they go. This is my reason for the how to develop streets smarts passage, which is to give readers strategical methods of keeping themselves and loved ones around them safer. Also being able to realize when someone or people are plotting violently against them and considering themselves as a predator and them the prey.

6ᵀᴴ PHASE

Process of
A Mental Rebirth

SELF-IMPROVEMENT

A mental rebirth means you are born into a new mentality, new life, new experiences, new healthy emotions, and a new destiny. A mental rebirth allows and give you the power to deal with and ultimately overcome past tragedies mental, emotional, and spiritual trauma's that still now frequently hunts you. This is the process: you must isolate yourself from the negativity of the world and focus on a positive transition. Peace and quit. Preferably not allowing anything to distract you. I suggest turn off the TV, radio, computer, gaming systems, and anything that can interfere with this process of self-improvement, new life, and cleansing. "Your mind is your cable box. You can tap into infinite channels without getting charged at any time," (Lemon). Put down the remote, turn off the TV, pick up your consciousness, and turn on your awareness. You must isolate yourself from everything that makes you miserable, weak, distracts you from strength, self-improvement and power. In order to go through this rebirth, you must slow down and slow your mind down. Anything that makes you rush detach from it for a while until you can gain more of your time back. Leave any environment that rushes you and controls your time. It is a powerful experience when you stand still and be patient. It takes time and patience in order to self-improve. You cannot self-improve if you never give time back to yourself by focusing on yourself. "The inside always reveals the truth through patience and stillness, while the outside always distracts you from the truth through rushing you," (Lemon). Accept first in your mind that you are moving on and promise yourself that you will not allow the past to continue to defeat you and make your life unhappy and miserable. Then mentally start fresh and think about positive thoughts and futuristic dreams and goals. You must replace those past negative thoughts with positive thoughts of inspiration. It can permanently cure you from these mental demons or it can paralyze these demons and slow them down depending upon each individuals mind strength and regulation. Either way your mind will be more clear to think and you will be much happier and at peace. You are placing yourself in the future by not thinking about the past. This is a strategy and a way to eventually give you strength to forget or learn to deal with these negative issues that's holding you back from greatness, happiness, peace, and financial success. It will teach you how to leave the past in the past and move on. The more you rely on the past you will never be able to move forward in a healthy and productive way. Stop focusing on the past, live for the future. All negativity directed toward you, turn positive. Take all constructive or deconstructive criticism positively. "Adapt to your mistakes, because they are just a way to help you better survive and improve,"(Lemon).

[DESTINY]

In The Beginning

"If you continue to follow the pattern of history, then your present and future thoughts are already predestined to provoke the same decisions and actions,"(Lemon).You cannot move forward if you do not know what is stopping you from moving forward. People go through life not knowing if they are actually going into the right direction, thinking in the right direction and a powerful direction. People go through life not knowing what actually started them off on their path of life and not knowing what piece they really are on the chess board. If you do not know what piece you are on the chess board, then you will have no idea of how to win the game! If you do not know what piece you are on the board, then you will not know how to move, when to move, and where to move. So, in order to win you must find out what piece on the board you are and then learn your moves, how to move, when and where to move. Then now you have the power to move in the places on the board where you were not predicted to and now you move spots that people wouldn't think you would. Now you control the game! Also people go through life not knowing if they are on a path of misguidance. You will find out if you are being misguided or if you are on a journey of misguidance by actually understanding the history of your misguidance, which is also the history and beginning of your life and is also the beginning and history of your individuality. Going back to the history of your misguidance. This is going back to the beginning of YOU. This sounds weird and contradictory, but just hear me out it will make sense once you understand it. In order to realize if you are misguided you must follow the path of your misguidance(of course now at this point you know you are misguided) so now you are just going back to the history of your misguidance in order to find out the root of your misdirection and how it came to be. You are not going backward if you are going backward for purposes to understand how to move forward. Once you get to the root and history of your misguidance, then you will understand how it all started and what began a life of misdirection out of controlness, and unhappiness. Now you will understand the core of your misdirection and now will have the power to change your destiny and not go through the same problems as you would have if you lived in the same destiny. You understand this now by actually going in the direction leading back to the start of what misguided you. Gain self knowledge, meaning going back to the origin of self. Remember your history is your beginning. History is the beginning. You must go back to the start of yourself in order to understand how you came to be and what you will possibly become. Going backward to move forward is much more honorable and powerful then continuing forward and still moving and backward. You will always find all answers and all truth in the beginning and going back to history or the start. You will always find all solutions and cures to anything by going back to the history of it and the history of anything is also the beginning of what will be. Where anything begins you will find all answers of how something will end. Go to your individual history to find out how you will possibly end. Remember you have the power to rewrite your own destiny, future history, and you have the power to rewrite your own ending to your own life. If everybody but you can predict what your destiny is, then they have more power over your life then you could ever imagine. This is a major problem. Nobody should have that power to know how your story will highly possibly end and you never had a clue of what direction you are going into.

[GAIN A DIFFERENT KNOWLEDGE]

Change your knowledge, which will reroute your destiny! Destiny is everything and knowledge is everything too. Whatever knowledge you are born into will initially lead you to who you will become, what you will become, what direction you will go, and how your life and destiny will play out. When you gain a different knowledge from what your destiny allowed, then you have rerouted your destiny and your legacy will change too. Also your history will be rewritten and will not be under the same determinants as your initial born destiny. Also the rules change when you redirect your destiny. You are not subjected to the same rules as before either. Gain a different knowledge besides the knowledge that you were born into. If everybody but you can predict what your destiny is, then they have more power over your life then you could ever imagine. This is a major problem, but the solution is to gain a different knowledge above what your planned destiny was in order to gain control over your destiny, life, and in reality yourself.

[DIVIDING LINE OF DESTINY]

(Reality Check)

I always wondered: what was the dividing line between ultimate financial success and ultimate financial failure? Happiness versus unhappiness? Survival versus death? I began to ponder why some people had much success financially and why others did not. For example how did some people becoming millionaires, billionaires, extraordinary scientists, innovators, successful actors, lawyers, professional athletes, and prestigious doctors? How did certain people acquire happiness and peace regardless of their social class? Why did some people fail at all that they did? Mental Imprisonment also creates the following that I call a five theory downhill series: Mind poverty, Followers of followers, Self-deprivation, No impulse, and a Negative mindset.

These questions will be answered within the five theory downhill series in the next passages.

FIVE THEORY DOWNHILL SERIES

Mind Poverty

I have five theories as to why some people are happy, at peace, and rich as opposed to unhappy and financially poor. My first theory is that people don't realize that their life is guided by the way that they have mentally allowed themselves to be viewed; psychological binding. It is how their mind views themselves, the world, and what they actually believe to be true. Which this view becomes their perspective, and then ultimately becomes their perception. If all you see around you is poverty sometimes that becomes all you know, because you haven't seen any different nor were you taught any different. So in reality, you are mentally and physically impoverished. Once you chose to think beyond and above poverty or your condition, now you have mentally escaped it and all you have to do now is physically turn it into a reality. In reality you have already made it an reality, because this is your new mentality, now you just have to transform your mentality into something you see physically. You have to see everything at every angle. You must always see the bigger aspect of the smaller picture. The Most important thing is **that you must see the big picture of you**! Because if you see the big picture, then you have more power to minimize your weaknesses as well as maximize your strengths.

FOLLOWERS OF FOLLOWERS

My second theory people who are trapped in mental imprisonment don't even got close to success is because they never really thought outside the box and freed their minds to think and always were followers of followers. They follow the same people that have the same perception that kept them limited and prevented them from gaining higher knowledge to become leaders. In addition they get advice from the same people who cannot lead them out of captivity. Ultimately it becomes a waist of focus and time. In addition these people were mentally restricted because they were intimidated by people because of who they were and what title, position, class level, age, and race they were. Furthermore, they were intimidated, because they gave these people to much mental power by giving them too much undeserved respect, which led to eventually putting these people on pedestals and ultimately practically worshiping them as if they were Gods. I'm not saying don't respect people, but it becomes a problem when you respect people more than you respect yourself. But the sad thing about it is they did not even realize that they gave people this mental power, which was one of the reasons why their minds were imprisoned.

SELF-DEPRIVATION

My Third theory is that sometimes it wasn't people that stopped their success and accomplishing their life dreams, it began to appear obvious that the person that they were intimidated by the most was themselves. This is why some people did not complete or even start the path of their dreams because they were scared and feared failure and most importantly they lacked courage and encouragement from within and from the ones they loved. Consequently, in reality these people already failed by not even trying, so failure was their destiny and fate, because they created that downfall. No one is to blame, but themselves. However ultimately, you cannot look for others to encourage you; you must find encouragement, inspiration, and motivation within yourself.

NO IMPULSE

In retrospect, back to the people who dreams were stuck at a truck pit stop, because first they gave up on themselves and lost self will, motivation, and self empowerment. Second, some allowed others to intimidate them, discourage them and stopped them from thinking toward happiness, greatness, and success. These people, who they allowed to intimidate them, were one of the reasons why their mental growth was stunted, limited and restricted from high levels. Third, it began obvious that their confidence levels were lower than the heart beat of a cadaver. Yes, as we all know or now know a cadaver is a deceased dead human. So it is safe to say their confidence levels were non living. 50 percent of themselves not believing in themselves sometime developed from people they loved who did not believe in them, doubted them, and indirectly or directly discouraged them. The other 50 percent was them themselves not believing in themselves and directly discouraging and doubting themselves. Also, if people they loved did not directly discourage them growing up, they still found ways of indirectly discouraging them. So you do the math, there was not even a one percent chance of them reaching greatness, following or living their dreams. I now believe that no encouragement is just as bad as discouragement.

(NEGATIVE MINDSET)

Fifth and last these people occupied a negative mindset as well, which clouded their judgment and consequently denied them the ability to have an open minded receptive approach to life. This negative mindset bonded them to a life of pain, suffering, agony, financial unsuccess, mental degeneration/disease, and unhappiness. Furthermore, this way of thinking forced them into years and even decades of setbacks and distractions. But if there is a way into something there is always a way out. But what's unfortunate originally it is not their fault most of the time that they initially began out in a massive downfall. This way out of thinking this way is too think just the opposite. For example, when someone gets bitten by a poisonous snake, the only cure and antibody is within the poisonous snake. The ultimate cure to change you is you!

Having a permanent negative mindset ultimately defeats ones dreams and breaks people down mentally and physically that leads to poor health and sooner than expected miserable life and death. A negative mindset stunts your maturity and puts a restriction on the development of power and limits your consciousness. Also it inhibits one to transcend to higher levels of themselves (a better you). My definition of a negative mindset is a corrupted and dark mindset either from birth that was inherited or developed or redeveloped through adolescence and teenage years into adulthood by outside variables by means of world influences, media influences, forced unhealthy limited perspectives, peer pressure, and environment. This negativity is produced by outside eyesight, which over powers the inside, which then now the outside lives from within. It is a mindset majority of useless and unproductive thoughts, ideas, reasoning, logic, and practicality. Ultimately creating your mind and mentally constructs your reality and world of rationale, comprehension, interpretation, understanding and beliefs, which sets the standards as what we see as normal and a way of life. Which this negative mindset of the world significantly demotes, deconstructs and inevitably leads one down a path of destruction, unhappiness, misery, and financial unsuccess. Typically, a negative mindset generates stress and stress generally creates depression and other mental diseases that ultimately ware your body down and people develop physical diseases later on in life that creates disease, mental pain, lower negative submissive and destructive feelings and thoughts like hate, agony, extreme stress and worry. Ultimate lowers life and happiness expectancy. For example, a negative mindset will lead to a person being overstressed, worried, and down and out. Being down and out can lead to depression and possibly suicide. Now you try to cope with your depression and go deeper into depression, because you have not yet dealt with what made you depressed in the beginning. In contrast you must agree that a positive mindset does not cause mental disease, stress and depression. A positive mindset enables people to be more encouraged and happy about life and gives you peace and relaxes or mind and body.

You must inspire yourself to begin to think on a whole different level of positivity that ultimately gives you the gift of clear thinking and mental freedom. It gives you mental independency that allowed your mind to be set free. In retrospect having a negative mindset will destine you for financial unsuccess, misery, defeat, and despair. It is safe to say by occupying this mindset you will never be loved or love someone like love was meant to feel. If you think about it love is something positive and good, so with a negative mindset of despair and bitterness, you will never get the full effect of love or give the full effect of it. But, consequently ultimately you have a high possibility of failing in all that you set out to do, because of how your thought process processes. Sometimes we are our own curse and we have no one to blame but ourselves. It a saying that goes, I made it against all odds. But, I think people can sometime be the one making those bad odds for themselves. Sometimes people can be their worst enemy themselves. Everything all starts up in your mind. A lot people don't even realize that it is them who needs to change and not everybody else. They will never change if they don't realize that they need too and they will be the reason of their own downfall and fatality. You cannot fix something that you have no idea that it is broke.

[REINVENT YOURSELF]

"Sometimes you must reinvent yourself. However, your reinvention should not be to the standards of people and the world, but to the high expectations and high standards of what you are truly capable of," (Lemon).

Sometimes you are what is holding you back from happiness, wealth, and greatness. "The code of life is to decode the original code, if it is destructive, and inscribe it with your true DNA," (Lemon). If your house was built on an unstable foundation eventually it will fall in due time. You eventually will have to bring in a demolition crew to destroy the house for reconstruction. Sometimes you have to reconstruct yourself, but to reconstruct yourself you must first realize that you have been destroyed. You can never know if you have been destroyed if you never put enough focus and time to realize such a problem.

It's weird to me when people say, "I am who I am and I am not changing for anyone." It's odd because, if the person you are today is not a happy, fulfilled, strong, successful, brave, and peaceful person how can you truly like who you are? Or how can you truly accept yourself being as discontent as you are? "Nobody will know what they need to be if they never saw the other side of what they should be, of what they should not be, and what they had the potential to become," (Lemon).

I know from experience and from being a human that we will not always be strong and in great spirits. However, wouldn't it be wonderful if you had something to turn to when needing a strength and spirit booster? Look no longer, you will find in my book inspiration even though the eyes of facing annihilation. "How do you know this is the person that you need to be now and in the future if you never had any control over the person you became," (Lemon)?

[LIMITATIONS]

"The side that you never knew existed is the same side that completes your existence,"(Lemon). Limitations will always keep you incomplete and not knowing your true power and potential. Limitations and restrictions will inevitably control your true abilities and will suppress a deeper understanding of who you really are and what you really can do and become. They will keep you only at a superficial and physical understanding. What you want is a inside and beyond an external view. What you want is two sides to every story. Going past what controls you or limits you will always give you two sides to a story and will always reveal the truth or another understanding beyond what you could not understand before. "If you accept the limitations that were placed on you, then you can not complain about not ever gaining power beyond what controls you,"(Lemon). The ones who go beyond the call of duty will always be the ones who push it beyond the limit. They will always be the ones who strive for perfection and will be the ones who will know what true happiness is, what true power is, what their abilities are, and what the true truth is. Because pushing it beyond the limit is another way of saying you are striving for perfection. Which striving for perfection and pushing it beyond its limits will always go beyond the limits of misery and will be going into the direction of GOD and any direction toward GOD will ensure happiness. They will always have a different and higher level of belief. They will always know and experience higher possibilities of what most might think is impossible. "If you do not have an open mind to what you believe then that will explain why there are limitations on what you can achieve,"(Lemon).

You only will achieve at the level of what you believe. They will always see their true purpose and will always be the ones who create their own destiny. Creating your own destiny means that you push it past the limit and you find your true purpose and existence. If you continue to live a limiting life, then you will never develop vision beyond what stops you from recognizing your full potential and power. "Once you push things beyond its boundaries and limits everything that you thought was magical, mythology, and a fantasy now becomes a reality,"(Lemon).

7ᵀᴴ PHASE

(Developing Definite Truth, Ultimate
Peace, Happiness, and Power)

[GOD]

The Creator
Spirituality

The creator known as God made us in his own image and gave us the power, knowledge, insight, intellect, wisdom, will, and strength to get through anything and conquer all obstacles even when failure seems inevitable. "I'm not usual, I'm very unusual, they call it being a rebel. But I just call it digging deep and that comes with breaking some of the rules when I speak," (Lemon). Even Jesus Christ himself was a rebel, because he did not follow the rules of ignorance, he did not believe or give into the knowledge of deception and manipulation, and he did not accept or live by the beliefs,laws, and rules of fear and limitation. You know how people say I need to find myself or I am lost. I believe we are all born found through a creation by GOD, but become lost, because we are born into a world of deep lies and deception. This means that they need to find the truth about themselves and what direction they need to go in. So in other words we are born into false truths that limits our deeper understandings and restricts us from knowing what we are truly capable of. I believe the ones who search and question the world will always find more truth, power, and get closer to GOD. Also the ones who understand that our existence is much deeper than the physical will always be much more stronger through awareness of how they need to be within a illusionist world. Those who know there is much more to our existence will always have a deeper understanding, which that above the boundary understanding will always allow them the access to the real and true truth of everything. However, I believe those who live in more truth then lies have a different type and level of pain. Its a deeper more painful pain. This painful truth can either make you or beak you, that is why they say the truth hurts. Because the deep truth can destroy your spirit and cause you to be emotionally and mentally traumatized which can cause you to lose your mind. Because it will be too much new and beyond your understanding of information processing too fast within your mind and brain. You can compare this process to a computer breakdown, shutdown, and vulnerability to viruses. You know how a computer will breakdown or will go really slow, because to much information at one time in a rapid pace beyond the speed of that computer will cause problems and setbacks due to an overflow of information. But this painful information will not cause pain of weakness; this pain turns into strength and power that GOD blesses them with from suffering so much to get to GOD and from going above and beyond the boundaries and into the unknown just to get the closest to how they need to be and what they really need to learn and understand and what not to waist their time on trying to understand. I believe you have no choice but to endure a lot of pain and suffering in order to understand what GOD really wants you to be and do. Also I believe you have no choice but to endure a lot of pain and suffering in order to understand the true power of compassion (just as JESUS felt). Once you reach the lvel of compassion, you are not subjected to live by any laws governed by anything physical. Christ lived by the Divine laws and rules of God and once you get to the level of compassion I believe you are now living in the divine realm of GOD!

(FREE WILL)

You will never have free will if you do not gain intelligence at the level or beyond the will of those who want to limit you. You will never have free will if you never understand the will of GOD. When you focus on the will of GOD then intelligence and freedom will come naturally. But if you do not understand the will of GOD you will never break free from the will of others. The will of GOD would want you to realize and understand who you truly are and what you are truly capable of. However, there are some who wish to control your freedom and their will is to take your freedom and keep you in the dark about who you should be and all the possibilities you can achieve. You will never have free will until you never break free from the will of others.

If your perspective, understanding, and perception is limited, then your will and you will be so far from being free. Expand your perception will expand your freedom and will power. Expand your perception, the less your will be controlled by those and things that does not want you to see and be free.

[DO NOT FEAR TO QUESTION?]

"You might be living in knowledge of lies and you wonder why you can't see or fly above the skies," (Lemon). What I mean is there is nothing wrong with questioning what you are living in or questioning what you believe. Sometimes the only reason you do not know the other side of what you do not know is because, you never challenged what you believe. In addition, sometimes you will realize the only reason you feared what you didn't know is because, you never challenged what you believed. When you challenge anything, there will always be two outcomes, either you will win or you will lose. However, in this case challenging what you believe, you cannot lose, you will always win. Because, either way you will find out more knowledge and you win every time you gain knowledge, whether on a losing side or winning side. In addition you have already loss and don't even know it, because you never challenged what you follow. You do not want to follow anything that will automatically put you in the position to loss and stay lost. You do not want to follow something that has every intention to lead you into the wrong direction or lead you into a deep whole of false knowledge and understanding. "If something did not mean what you thought it meant, then that would change the whole understanding of the content,"(Lemon).

God gave us the mental ability to reach elevated levels of intellect, knowledge, strength, and capability that will insure happiness, peace, greatness, financial success, and riches. Also, God gave us these abilities for us to develop extreme never before seen physical strength and mental strength, which is acquired through developing a strong mind, strong heart, and will. This gives you the courage and confidence of the Spartans, like in the movie 300! In addition God provided us with the mental capability to reach higher levels of consciousness, understanding, and realities. "You cannot truly or fully practice and become what you believe in, if you live within a reality that will not allow you to fully experience what you want to become,"(Lemon).

However, God blesses us with these abilities but it is up to each individual person to tap into these abilities and gifts. To maintain this disconnection for mental imprisonment you must keep your focus fresh through discipline and practice. However, you must pray to God for becoming what God wants us all to become, which is greatness, happiness, and peace! However, my philosophy is, "A prayer can only go so far as to what you most of the time focus on," (Lemon). Meaning how can you expect God to bless you and give you what you ask and pray for if you do not give God enough of your focus and time in regards to what you ask for. In addition how do you expect to receive a blessing that you do not put enough of your own focus and time into the same thing you pray for? We must have faith that God will deliver us from crippling situations. However, "Faith without taking action is hopeless," (Lemon).

[THE TRUTH]

Purpose

"We all are made perfect, but are imperfections are placed and forced on us by the world," (Lemon). Ultimately its up to you to not accept what is forced on you. You still have a choice rather to accept something or not. So, why would you accept your imperfections if you understand you were not the cause of them, so in reality they are not your imperfections, because you did not create them, so on a deeper note why would you accept imperfections that wasn't even created by you? Or why would you accept becoming and being somebody, someone, or something that is not your fault? Why would you accept being something that is so far from and the complete opposite of who you was originally created to be? So accepting something that is really not suppose to be anyway will always lead you into the wrong and opposite direction of where you originally thought you were going. Do not accept anything that will take strength and power away from you. Accepting imperfections will always lead you into a powerless and misguided direction.

We all are made in GODS image. So if we are created in GODS image, then we all are mad perfect. We all are created in perfection. However, the world redesigns are original fabrication, which in turns transforms us into imperfect beings. These imperfections recreate who you were (which was perfect), who GOD created you to be and all come from whatever circumstances you are born into and subjected too. "You are only a product of your imperfections, only if you allow your mistakes determine who you become," (Lemon).

[PURPOSE]

Part 2
(Change)

We all need to change, once we are intoxicated by the world that surrounds us. Once you realize that you once were perfect, but this world formed your imperfections and you still choose not to change, then you are letting GOD and yourself down just by knowing such a powerful knowledge. Also you are not giving yourself a chance to experience a more powerful you, a stronger you, a healthier you, and a more intelligent you. You receive all that I just mentioned by striving for the original perfect you that GOD created you from the start to be. In order to get back to where GOD in the beginning created us all to be(which is perfect), is by being committed to striving for perfection. Striving for perfection means that you must change. It means that you give yourself no other choice but to change and strive toward power that GOD puts inside you. Striving for perfection means that you are going into the most powerfulist direction you could ever go. Which is the direction toward GOD, toward finding yourself, your spirit, your soul, gaining complete health, strength and truth. If you never changed especially considering the fact that GOD made us in GODS image, which is perfection, still keeping in mind that we are born into an imperfect world that stripes away the very essence of what GOD originally made us to be, how could you not make a choice to decide to rededicate your life to striving for perfection and striving to change back toward GOD and your true original powerful self? We are all born into an out of control world. Where there is possibility for anything to be out of control, then there will always be imperfection, weakness, and desperate measures for change and reconstruction. To gain more control and to steer yourself into the direction of perfection you must gain self-knowledge. Again in order to reach higher levels of perfection toward your original self, you must gain self-knowledge, which self-knowledge gives you control, and now you have the ability to change toward what GOD created you as. Self-knowledge is a lower level form of GOD knowledge. You cannot change, gain control, or strive for a higher you without first knowing knowledge of self. If you do not gain any knowledge beyond what an imperfect world gives you, then you will be so far from the image of perfection and power of what GOD created you to be. If you do not change you will be so far from the truth, higher understanding, mental/emotional health, and survival. Only the strong survive, this is true and only the strong survive, because they constantly adapt to change. If you never knew yourself, then you never have had any control of yourself. Being born as I said into an imperfect and out of control world, what makes you think you are who you need to be, or that you have your sanity, or ever had it considering you never knew yourself? Also being born into a out of control world, a imperfect world, a world of deception, and not ever knowing yourself, what makes you think you ever had any control over who you became and where your destiny leads? Striving for perfection will help you maintain your power, your sanity, or even better it will help you get it back. Because striving for perfection means that you are now going back into the direction of GOD and any direction toward GOD will inevitably give you power and will surely be a route toward perfection and your true self. Also striving for perfection will bring you purpose and happiness!

[PURPOSE]

Part 3
Service

"Service gives you purpose and fulfillment within a world of hopelessness," (Lemon). We all were put on this Earth to provide service for each other. Service is one of our purposes, because when you do it, it will replace a void in your life that I believe produces a healing effect. I believe that when you service and help others, you are helping them heal, grow, develop, prosper and you are or will get all of that back in return. You will get back 100 more times what you have given when you begin to help others accomplish something. Service creates a deeper meaning to life. When you help others you gain a special place in GODS heart and when you gain a special place in GODS heart you will be given all you desire and could ever wish or hope for. You will never find true purpose within anything physical or anything created after GODS design. Your purpose will always be beyond what you can see. This is why there is only short-term gratification and satisfaction in anything that you cannot see. However, there is long-term purpose, gratification, glorification, meaning, and happiness in putting all your energy into anything internal and anything that will bring out the best in those who you help and provide service for.

[THE PHYSICAL IS NOT THE TRUTH]

How can a child of GOD ever connect to GOD and GODS energy and power if they have never saw the world through the perspective as GODS only son experienced it? Christ did not see the world through the eyes of the physical. Christ saw the world through spiritual lenses. You cannot connect or communicate with GOD on a higher level without first realizing and understanding that the physical world is not the truth. If you do not get this concept, then you will be forever easily controlled or manipulated by the forces of the physical realm and deception will be what you will always live in.

"You will always have limited and superficial experiences if you continue to allow external variables to be the architect of your core belief system,"(Lemon).

This view will always trick your eyes to believe all external aspects to be true and will persuade you to accept as face value. It is said by most people I will not believe it until I see it. This is not the best way to gain higher consciousness or truths that God wants you to see beyond what is distributed to you from the physical transferring through the eyes. The eyes can only process what is already there. But to process information that is not physically based you must go to the bottom, which the bottom is always internal and what is not superficially seen. They say the eyes are our window to our souls. If this is true, then how can you connect to your soul and understand the true power of it, if you continue to allow physical components to control the very existence of you? I believe words are our inside connection to spirituality and God, but numbers are our connection to the physical and materialistic world.

[THE EYES ARE LIES]

"You will never know what it means to be alive if you continue to allow what you physically see create your vision and perception of what truly is,"(Lemon). Never allow your eyes to create your reality of truth. The eyes will always separate you from real truth. The eyes will never give you true truth and if you never experienced true truth, then you can not feel the power being truly alive. The way that you connect to real truth is by allowing your perception to be recreated by The eyes will always prevent you from going deep to find the most important answers to the most important question, which is the power of why. The why are true knowledge, power, and understanding. If you never search for and find the why, then you will forever be stuck in a false physical reality of the unknown. The eyes will only process information from the physical. You will never experience true power and understanding if you continue to see the world as it is given to you. In order to see past the eye of the physical, you must go inside, you must go deep. Going deep is the only way to the true truth. It is the only way you will get to the bottom of the truth. The true truth is never at the top of anything. If you never have digged deep, then you will never find the true truths and you will forever live in lies that come across as truths. Real truth and living is always found inside and the eyes are blind to the internal until attention is refocused and eyes are repositioned to look within instead of believing everything physical that you see. The eyes are blind and cannot process an understanding that requires a less illusionary controlled mind and an unbreakable spirit in order to survive through what GOD wants you to see and reveal to you. You cannot receive what GOD wants to reveal to you if you continue to see the world through the lenses of the physical. Nor will you ever be able to process GODS message and what GOD tries to relay to you if you accept the world as it is given to you. Nothing is free in this world, so why would you expect the truth to be free considering it is the most powerful thing in this world? Because who ever has the most truth has the most power on Earth. Also the most powerfulist thing in the world(the truth) will always be the hardest to attain looking at it from an external view(I'll explain). People who live to control will do what ever it takes to make sure ultimate truth will never be revealed to you. They will make sure they deceive you by giving you a false perception that tricks your eyes into making you believe what you see is actually the truth. They will do what ever it takes to keep the truth about even your own self away from you.(Explaining from up above) Strive for perfection and GOD will reveal unto you the real truth about yourself. Which any way of striving for perfection will always start a journey searching from within. Any voyage from within will give you a face to face encounter with GOD. Which GOD will reveal unto you your true self, which this true truth is free of charge. Because GOD sees it as you have paid the price of gaining this truth by not being deceived by the lies and that is more then enough for GOD to give you back what was already yours in the beginning. Which is the gift of you and the secret to knowing who you really are, who you really are not, and what you are truly capable of. However any knowledge that you find outside of you can easily be set up to misinform you and misguide you into the direction of deeper lies, false knowledge, and separating yourself further and further away from what you were truly created to be. So in actuality you are a lie, but do not know it until you realize that there is a much more truer, better and powerfuler you that has been kept secret. This is why you continue to feel lost, because you are so far from a truer you and GOD and anywhere GOD is true truth is. To become true and to get closer to GOD you must strive for perfection, which will reveal unto you YOU, true knowledge, which will give you the ability to distinguish between what is real, what is fake, what is true and what is a lie. So in reality you are fake(not your fault)until you find your true self that GOD created you to be. There is no reason to be ashamed of what you did not know about being. So a lot of things that you see that is promoted to be free, it is safe to say it is most likely not the truth. Just as free knowledge doesn't mean that it is true knowledge. Don't accept everything that is given unto you especially realizing that you must pay for everything in this world, even true knowledge. To validate real true knowledge to be accurate you must research, get to the bottom of it, which means you have to go back to the beginning, origin of it, and the source. GOD blesses people in abundance who commits to researching the truth. A researcher for GOD will always have the most power in the world and will retreieve the lost power and truth of themselves and the world, because that person will always be lead back into the direction of GOD and true power.

[SPIRITUAL INTERPRETATION VS. SUPERFICIAL PERCEPTION]

Superficial Perception
(The 6 Senses)

What is the true truth and the real truth behind a false perception that you believe to be true? What you superficially see is what creates your perception. A lot of peoples believes are formed by what they physically and superficially perceive to be true or real. Which this perception is developed by the six senses of eyesight, touch(feel), hearing, smell, taste, and . . . . I consider this interpretation of reality a belief based off a superficial perception. However in this passage I will be discussing the sense of eyesight. Anything belief or perception constructed by a superficial interpretation will never lead you to a deeper connection toward GOD,the realm of Spirituality,and true truth. A superficial perception is created by a physical understanding and acceptance of what is and is only the half of it. Once this surface understanding of what you see is accepted this superficial and physical perception becomes true and becomes the end of what you will know. Most people say I will not believe it until I see it. This acceptance of this belief is the reason why you will not develop sight beyond what you do not know or understand. Also this is why your experiences will be limited to only what you accept and believe to be it. The surface is not the end nor is it the beginning. To always get to the bottom of something you must go deep within it. Anything deep is never superficial or on the surface. So never accept a superficial perception to be it, the beginning, or the end.

"The most powerful are the ones who do not accept what is free or given, because they understand what is free does not promise freedom,"(Lemon).

[SPIRITUAL INTERPRETATION]

How do you find the true truth behind your perception of what you believe to be true?

The true truth can only be retained through a Spiritual Interpretation. Which a Spiritual Interpretation will give you healing knowledge. You can not acquire healing knowledge through any physical or superficial perception, because they represent illusions of freedom and truth. A way you find the truth behind your perception of what you believe to be true is by believing beyond what you superficially see. Which that belief will form a deeper and truer perspective, which I call Spiritual Interpretation. The definition of Spiritual Interpretation—True truth, healing knowledge, and information formed and collected by believing beyond what you superficially and physically see.

A

(SPIRITUAL AWAKENING)

The way you become spiritual and have a spiritual awakening is by believing beyond what you physically and superficially see. Which will grant you true freedom and open up opportunities that wasn't available before. This freedom and opportunities arise from not allowing your beliefs to be constructed by superficial perceptions. When you do not allow your views to be created by superficial perceptions you will be offered a spiritual perspective, knowledge, power, and healing abilities beyond this world. Superficial perception is what controls your ability to heal and closes the door for any entry for GOD to heal you and show you how to heal. In order to experience a spiritual awakening first you must stop allowing your beliefs to be formed and controlled by superficial perceptions. When you allow your beliefs to be constructed by physical perceptions you can not understand things deeper and above your head. For example, THE BIBLE has spiritual concepts and understanding way beyond this universe, which was created by GOD and men just were the messangers and writers that they got word from GOD to create the BIBLE. So you have people who believe in the BIBLE, but do not really understand it, because these are spiritual concepts thought of by GOD and are way above our understanding. So why would you think you would ever understand the BIBLES powerful spiritual literature and knowledge from GOD through a belief system that you developed from a superficial perception? This is why you can not understand concepts and knowledge above your understanding. GOD is no where near Earth remember, so just by understanding this concept, you must admit there is no way you can believe you will understand GODS word from a Earthy perception! Also to become spiritual and understand GODS word completely you must have a spiritual awakening. This awakening can only happen when there is a shift of attention from physical attractions toward internal realization. Why would you expect to understand something spiritual and become spiritual if your attention is controlled by everything superficial? I just used the BIBLE for a more relatable subject, but the bottom line is the BIBLE is a knowledge and understanding that is beyond a superficial realm of realization. So your understanding is limited, because you have superficial and earthy beliefs. How could you believe that you will understand the content and concepts of the BIBLE by just perceiving through your regular senses that only create superficial perceptions and understanding? "To acquire and understand truth beyond this world, you can not live on the surface,"(Lemon).

(FORGIVENESS)

You must forgive yourself for what ever happened and you must forgive others. You must let go. Letting go completely means not allowing whatever is hurting or controlling you to live in side you. You must not submit to the negative emotions as guilt, regret, and shame. These emotions will keep you stuck in the past and you will not be able to move on with a clear mindset. You must ask God to forgive you and you must forgive yourself as well as others. Which God has already forgiven you because you had a change of mind and heart and will be given the gift of redemption. After that mental transition happens, you now have had a positive mental rebirth. Now you must move forward and not allow your past negativity to corrupt your positive bright future plans. For example, within the movie Men in Black, the agents always used this hand-held little gadget to zap the memories of the aliens they questioned. They did this so they would not remember the past. After going through this rebirth it will give you the power of a fresh start with old commissaries, enemies, family, co-workers and forgotten friends that you were the reason of segregation. It will give you a new mindset of fresh breath to redeem yourself among people who have hurt. In a way you can look at them like it's a new beginning and you are just meeting them.

Forgiveness is another powerful way to take the negative care away, stress, and future worry. Forgiveness is Power and gives you ultimate control back over how you felt in the past and how you will feel in the future. Forgiving allows you to release all those emotions of haunt such as hate, regret, guilt, and shame. Once you truly forgive you completely are letting go of the past and whatever affected you at that time. It takes inner strength and power to forgive. However, it is worth every bit of strength. When you do it, you will feel like living again. It gives you the power back to move and think forward! If you never forgive you never will be truly happy or at peace. If you do not forgive you will always have a feeling of vulnerability. Vulnerability submits you to feel like the victim.

[VULNERABILITY]

Vulnerability is one of the highest levels of weakness. Thinking you are vulnerable will only make you feel like you are vulnerable. This is one of the highest levels of weakness! Thinking and feeling like you are the victim will indefinitely make you feel and look like you are defeated. Feeling vulnerable disables you from any control or power that you once had. Vulnerability alone will put you in a category of being the prey. Feeling vulnerable will submit you to a lifetime of insecurity, unhappiness, and misery. It will be hard to give yourself to someone and love someone like love was truly meant. Also it will be difficult for you to let someone love you just as much. To detach from this feeling you must forgive and let go. You have to release hate from your mind, heart, spirit, and soul. This is the only way to gain control and power back. You must realize it is not your fault, because number one when you are vulnerable, you have no control what so ever as to what is happening or happened. You must really understand when someone is vulnerable they are at their weakest and they have no fight in them or control. So whatever has happened to you, do not blame yourself and it is not your fault.

Also it is very important that you do not replay back in your mind those negative memories. Remember to never be ashamed or feel guilty from any a situations that you could not control. Negative shame and guilt are the main emotion that complete vulnerability and submits you to live as a helpless victim. When you release shame, guilt, hate, let go, and you forgive this is when you will feel a feeling of rejuvenation. You will feel a feeling of peace, clear thinking and no worries regarding that situation. You will gain strength back. Ultimately this is when you gain your control and power back! I know that it is harder said than done. However, you must forgive all that trespassed against you. You must eventually forgive all that was involved. You even have to forgive the ones that was your protector. You must remember when you were at your weakest by being vulnerable. This took all control and power from you. Also remembering you was in a situation where you did not know what was going on, you did not know the facts of the situation, so in reality you had no way of knowing how to approach, respond, or control any of those situations. So all that what I just mentioned put you in a league of vulnerability, being powerless, and not able to gain any control. Just off of those facts alone none of what happened is your fault. So there is no need to hate yourself, have shame, or guilt. Imagine your protector with the same odds against him or her. They did not know what was going on with you and they did not know the facts of the situation. So your protectors approach and response was just as limited as yours was. Ultimately they had just as much as control and power as you, which was none. Just by that alone puts them in a league of vulnerability as well. Because it was impossible for them to help you by having no idea that you needed rescue. You can't hate them. Hate is also one of the highest levels of weakness, it is not power! "Hate is not power, it is one of the highest levels of weakness. Think about it, every day of every minute of every hour your mood is sour," (Lemon).

FEELINGS OF HAUNT

(Hostage of the Past)

Some feelings of haunt are negative regret, guilt, and shame. However, there is a way to release these hurtful, harmful, and extremely damaging emotions. Whatever is negatively mentally affecting you, haunting you, and bringing you down is going to destroy you if you allow it too. You must accept what is haunting you and detach from denial. You must defeat denial. Denial in itself will haunt you. You have to mentally detach and emotionally disconnect from the care that is negatively haunting you. This will detach the emotion and feeling of that thought. Ultimately detaching that emotion and feeling of that thought will release the care, pain, hurt, haunt, and will set you free from being a hostage of the past.

(HEAL YOUR MIND)

Memory Re-imprinting

Remember to remember your memory is your history. Your history is your past and your past are all memories o your history. So why not leave your past in history if it creates misery, pain, and suffering? You can heal your mind by changing your memory. Also growing means you have new memories. You must replace bad memories with good ones. You are basically replacing old memories with new ones. Your memories are your history. So your history controls your future and gives insights and previews of how you will be and how you will spend your time in the future. By changing and gaining new perspectives of old memories this will reform your history and memory. Which will create a different future, will create a shift in focus, attitude adjustment, your time will be spent different, because you changed your memories history. Ultimately your destiny and attitude will be rerouted into a different direction. "Never believe anyone's predictions of your future, unless you never took the time out to look at your past from a different perspective,"(Lemon).

Heal your mind through changing your memory of past mental and emotional traumatic experiences, which will eventually rewrite your past. In order to move forward you must go back to deal with those traumatizing experiences that leaves you with painful memories. It is better to deal with your past head on, then to think you have left it within the past by simply ignoring it. But you have not got over these past painful memories, because you live in them every day. The process of changing your memory means to gain a new perspective about that past traumatizing experience. Which this new perspective will change your memory of what that traumatizing past experience means and how it feels when you think of it in the future. That new meaning by the process of forming a new perspective of a past traumatizing experience will help you mentally and emotionally heal by means of now remembering through a new memory of what that past traumatizing situation means now. Just by thinking about a past situation different from before will change the way your memory remembers that situation. Other way to explain it is by thinking about a situation different from how you thought about it before will alter how you remember that situation. Ultimately this will give you a new memory of this past painful experience and will allow you to heal and gain more power back in regards to how you feel about this situation. Inevitably this perspective will change your overall perception, which will create a new and healthier experience that will allow you to release emotions of haunt. Emotions of haunt and pain such as shame, guilt, hate, and regret. For example, within my motivational chapter, when I tell my story about how my usb drive did not reach the destination and got thrown away like trash. This was my greatest achievement thus far within my life. This was my most precious and most cherished project. This was something I created, the first thing I ever really been as disciplined and dedicated to accomplishing. This was the first thing that I put the highest level of inspiration in. Unfortunately my whole life's work was thrown in the garbage as if it was nothing. At the end of that chapter I have a quote where I say "I'm thankful for my misery, I'm thankful for my suffering, I'm thankful for my hell, I'm thankful for my pain, and now I realized my lost became my biggest gain,". To make a long story short I had a tragic situation that actually was traumatizing to me. This experience left me with painful memories that played back and back again within my mind. So, in order for me to move on to finish my book I had to gain new inspiration. Ultimately I took that painful situation and changed my perspective of that experience, which altered that bad and negative memory toward a memory that gave me a new positive experience of that circumstance.

I gained higher motivation and inspiration through a past memory of termination. I changed a bad memory to a positive one by altering my perspective of that situation. I turned misery and pain into strength and healing.

[REMEDY FOR TRUE HEALING]

part 2
Honesty=Understanding=Healing

The remedy for true healing is always traced back to finding the truth. However to find the truth and to understand your problem you must be honest. Once you are honest you will find a solution and you will heal. In order to find the truth, gain control, healing, cures, moving forward, altering your destiny, gaining happiness, and solutions to any problems you must go back to the history and beginning of what ever it is that is out of control or discoursed or diseased, which the ultimate remedy with all of what I mentioned before is first being honest. Through honesty you will find true understanding and through understanding you will heal and be able to move on toward happiness. This is the remedy for mental and emotional healing and restoration.

(PEACE ISN'T FREE)

Everything in this world comes with a cost even peace and freedom. Everything in this world takes time to develop, even peace of mind. But, out of the two I would rather have peace then freedom any day. Because I believe you can still have peace and not be free. Just as much you cannot be free, but still have peace. Peace is a state of mind. Freedom to me is something that was taken from you, and then is given back to you. Which taking anyone's freedom initially effects their peace. However, through the mist of that freedom being taken, you can still acquire peace even considering your freedom was stripped away. You find that peace from within. "Nobody can take anything from you that you will not allow them to control," (Lemon). Freedom is physical, but peace is mental. If you find peace, to me this means you are free in every way. Once you gain peace your mind is free. If you can find peace without freedom, then you know you are truly happy. So, whatever you are going through, find peace and it will set you free. Peace will not find you, you must go get it.

(LIVING WILL!)

Put yourself in the perspective of a dying cancer patient and the doctor told you that you have 5 months to live. What would you care about? Who would you care about? Where would you go? Who would you spend your time with? What would you focus on? After putting yourself within the perspective of a cancer patient and answering all of those questions, then and only then you realized that it had to take you to force yourself within a dying cancer patients circumstances just to realize that you were never living or alive in the first place. Ask yourself will you live before you die? I believe we all need to make a will while being alive! A will that gives us more will power to do what it takes to achieve our dreams. A will that specifies what we need to be happy and at peace. We need to make a will for ourselves that benefits us individually while we are living. What is the point of living if we cannot benefit from our own lives? We tend to only make a will before we die for our loved ones who will only benefit from our death. But how about you benefiting from your own death before you die? "The main benefactor of your death should be you and the main benefactor of your life should be you within the process of living it," (Lemon).

(TIME TRAVEL)

Everyone is always tired. Either tired from work, school, kids, co-workers, family, friends, spouses, etc. I never heard anyone say I am tired, because of me. In other words, it's rare to hear someone say I am tired, because I put so time and work on myself. I say that to say this, too much of our time is controlled by everything and everybody but ourselves. Then we wonder why time flies. It only flies, because we individually are not the pilot of our plane. Don't go through life without ever being the pilot of your own plane. Take control at least of some of your time. If you do not, you will always be a passenger of your own life, which means you will rarely go to destinations that you want to go to. Ultimately when the pilot lands, then your time will be up. In other words when the plane lands is compared to when it is time for you to go. You do not want to leave out of this world going places that you never desired to go nor do things that you never desired to do. You do not want to land at your final destination with memories that you did not control at all. You do not want to be in the position to only say you traveled to places that you had no intentions of going. When you have more control over your time, you are freer. Which means you are happier. The more you control you take from time, the more life you gain back to live. From every breath you take, time shouldn't be the cause of you always being tired, miserable, and stressing. "Don't waste your time. Sometimes make time lose it's breathe and wait for you. Because time will surely find away to waste you," (Lemon).

[FOCUS IS POWER!]

"If you feel like things are falling apart and you believe things are falling apart, then this is enough reason to believe that it is. Which this is now the time to gain back control over your focus," (Lemon).Whatever you focus on most of the time will either will offer you peace, happiness, and freedom or will control you or put fear into you. The most important idea is whatever you focus on most of the time is what ultimately guides your thoughts. Whatever you focus on most of the time will either submit you to high levels of weakness, suffering, fear, hurt, worry, misery, destroy your spirit, prohibit better attitudes, lowers energy, mental/emotional pain, and will overall break you completely down. Or whatever you focus on most of the time will present you with high levels of confidence, strength, clear thinking, high spirits, great high levels of energy, shining attitudes, courage, peace, happiness, freedom, and power. Now I am sure that you understand what you focus on most of the time is extremely important. How do you expect to reach higher levels of feelings if you never change your focus? It might be time to refocus and reroute your focus from misery toward a great legacy. Your focus is a force behind your attitude as well. Your attitude determines your altitude. If you shift your focus, then your attitude will shift, and ultimately your energy will shift, which will make you feel better. Remember we are massive amounts of energy. So if your energy is never up and high, analyze your focus. Change your focus; change your attitude, which will give you more control over your energy. "You cannot acquire powerful energy, while maintaining a focus of misery," (Lemon).

(TIME IS FOCUS AND FOCUS IS TIME)

Your focus is your time and your time is your focus. Never waste your time focusing on anything that is not worth your time. So take a good look at your focus and then you will know why you have been wasting your time and life. You might realize that you where focused on all the wrong things. You might uncover that you have been focusing on everything that made you weak, unhappy, and powerless. You might notice that you have been in your situation for long a long period of time, because you have not focused beyond that situation.

"No one can take action toward or control anything that is not within the boundaries of what they perceive or nothing that is beyond the perimeters of their focus," (Lemon).Take control of your focus and then your life and everything else will follow your focus. Once you control your focus, then your perspective will follow as well.

(MEDITATION)

Law of Attention

Your attention will either make you or break you! The law of attention is a very profound way of controlling your attention through meditation and altering your focus in order to reroute your destiny. The process of the law of attention is created and starts through guiding and commanding your focus to become more concerned with detail and monopolizing on your ability to concentrate on what forms your focus, because this is what controls your attention. The law of attention will give you the ability to repair and fix inside consistent emotional and detrimental problems, while refocusing your focus on solutions and leading your thoughts forward towards whatever you desire to manifest. Which by meditating your focus on what you want to manifest will ensure stability of confidence, health, happiness, and purpose. Meditating through the law of attention reveals and activates the minds true plasticity, enhances consciousness, en heightens awareness, and power of silence, peace, stillness, which puts you in a realm where time is not a controlling factor. It forces you to gain a different perspective on how powerful your attention really is. The law of attention shows you how to focus on your own attention and uncovers to you what is controlling your attention. This meditation gives you the opportunity to gain more control over your thoughts. Also going deep and meditating within the law of attention and then coming out of the law of attention will bring forth to you all that inhibits your progress, happiness, strength, capabilities, possibilities, success, greatness, power, spirit, and peace. In addition by you bringing your attention in focus and gaining new perspectives of everything negative that causes your misery. Then now you know what you need to focus your attention on in order to bring health, strength, reduction of stress, and worry.

(WHAT HAPPENS IN VEGAS STAYS IN VEGAS)

You must leave the past in the past. What ever happened in the past is in the past and you must move on. For example, relate this process of moving on to the saying, "What Happens in Vegas Stays in Vegas." You must get to the point of realizing it is what it is and you cannot travel backward to change it, so by thinking backward that is the only way you are keeping this issue alive. If you do not leave the past in the past it will only become a distraction in the near future and distant future. Also this will consume majority of you, which will make you insecure. Then this insecurity will be the reason you are miserable, unhappy, can't move on and destroy all dreams, future relationships, friendships and inspirations. You must move on mentally, if you don't you will suffer. I do not what anyone to stay in Vegas if you were visiting, unless of course you love to gamble or you enjoy, well I will not go there(laughing).

(WALKING FORWARD/ LOOKING BACKWARDS)

If you think about it looking and dwelling on the past never brings nothing good. Looking within the past only brings misery, stress and despair. I really believe human psychology that was created by God is in scripted and programmed for us to think ahead toward the future. For example, when a person is walking down the street looking forward, they can see everything in front of them and they know what to expect in terms of traffic, trains, buses, dogs, and other people. Basically they can see a lot of the dangers that's coming their way. However, imagine them walking forward and looking backward, for starters by looking back and walking forward after a while they will get a crook or cramp in their neck, (laughing). Because the body's anatomy and physiology of the body is not made to do such movements for long periods of time and not be uncomfortable. Furthermore, walking forward and looking backward in the same situation walking down the street a person will be now very much highly to be in the mist of the dangers they once was aware of and sooner than later have a accident. Also unfortunately eventually lose their life to the dangers they once was aware of, but became very susceptible to considering they were walking forward, but looking back. Think and look forward, unless you want an everlasting crook in your neck or you want to run into parked car with a sticker that says people that walk forward, but look backward will most likely run into parked cars and baby strollers, (laughing).

(THINK HAPPINESS!)

In the pursuit of happiness you will always have a purpose and with happiness there is always hope and with hope you will always have control over your life. "It is better to be happily crazy, then insanely mad," (Lemon).Staying more positive than negative is a very essential to gaining definite peace and happiness. For example, for a week every day I asked a co-worker how are you doing? Also I would say isn't the weather great today? My co-worker would say I am doing terrible, this is a horrible day, I hate this job, and the weather could be better. I would say to her, "I am doing great; everything is great and is only going to get better!" However, for five days in a row my co-workers responses were all negative and depressive conversation. My point is it has come to a time where being happy is not normal. People now look at you like something is wrong with you for being happy or smiling and better yet even ask you what's wrong with you? It is sad when people who are the healthiest mentally get questioned about their sanity by people who are the closest to insanity and are the most disturbed. Sometimes a good way to think more positive is to force yourself into thinking positive even when you do not feel like it. "At least try to trick yourself into being happy, because it appears we constantly trick and force ourselves into being miserable without even trying,"(Lemon).

If you notice people that are more negative are a lot more miserable, stressed, less successful, doubtful, and down in out. When you start your day out read something that encourages you, inspires, you, and motivates you. Read it so it can be engraved within your subconscious mind, so you can redevelop your conscious mind. Sometimes read it out loud. Also read it throughout the day if you need too. Then, before you go to sleep read it or say it out loud to store it within your subconscious mind and dreams. I figure what is the harm in starting your day out and ending your day out with processing motivation, encouragement, inspiration, and determination. The key is to reverse your mindset from negative and doubtful to positive and empowerment. A lot of people say get rich or die trying. "I say get happy or die trying," (Lemon)! Because if you focus on getting rich before happiness, you might find yourself trying to buy happiness. We must make happiness our number one priority and designate it a need and not a want. We need to say I need to be happy and not I want to be happy.

GROWTH

(Worries)

How can not develop, grow, and mature if you constantly worry about the same things? The answer is it is not possible to grow and mature if you most of the time worry about the same things that you worried about 1, 2, or 3 years ago. You cannot reach higher perspectives of maturity if you are stuck within rehabilitating worries. If you maintain the same worries as you did a year or two years ago, you will never have time to focus on growing, maturing, and won't be able to develop new thoughts of opportunities. Figuratively speaking, worry up, do not worry down. If your worries are the same as they were five years ago, ask yourself really is that growth and maturity? Your worries are what subject you to stay within those mindsets that stunts growth. Your worries are what become who you are to a certain extent. "You cannot become anything better then what you submit yourself to worry about," (Lemon). In other words you eventually become what you worry about.

[CHOOSE]

"Choose, stay confused, lost, or without a clue, and not knowing what to do," (Lemon). Make your mind up. It is said that if you do not stand for something, then you will fall for anything. If you stay without something to stand for then you will not have direction, vision, or leadership. You will be easily manipulated and controlled by those who prey upon you. A person who never makes their mind up is always confused, lost, and do not know how to make decisions that benefits them. Make your mind up to stand for something that will present you with honor, courage, dignity, respect, loyalty, and integrity. Make your mind up and stand for something that keeps you strong, happy, fearless, and peaceful. Once you make your mind and to stand on things of this nature, then when someone brings you everything that you don't stand for or brings you everything that you made your mind up not to stand for, then you have already created an automatic defense system. This system is a positive defensive automatic alert system formed from when you originally made your mind up in regards to what you decided to stand for and on. If anyone crosses your network of what you stand for, then it will be a natural instinct now for you to recognize this as a breach to your focus, peace, happiness, and direction. "You cannot think past anything, gain any vision, nor develop direction without first making your mind up," (Lemon).

[STICK TO IT]

"Always stick to what makes you sure of yourself. Which means your mind is made up until you get a higher moment of clarity, which is even better,"(Lemon).Ultimately you have to find one thing to stick to, make your mind up to, and stand for. Of course for purposes of not keeping your mind closed, you can add on to what you stand for and make changes when necessary. However, the goal is to train yourself to lead yourself, because when it is all said and done you make the final decision. People who do not stand for anything, it is much easier for them to trust anybody. Those who trust everybody without ever consulting themselves, nine times out of ten do not even trust themselves. If you can never trust yourself through your own consultation, then you can easily be misguided. This is why you must stand firm on what you make your mind up too and you must believe in what you make your mind up too as well. A person, who never stands their ground for nothing, cannot possibly stand for anything. You must become disciplined in, practice, and train for what you choose to stand for and make your mind up to. You must be very particular as to what you make your mind up to stand for, because this is what will guide you toward your future. This is what will determine how you will think in the future. I believe that there are too many people who are to critical and have negative opinions directed toward how other people think. In many cases they tell them that this is the wrong way to think. But, how could it be the wrong way to think if it is bringing someone more peace, happiness, success, joy, and is healing their mind, spirit, and soul from suffering and pain. While on the other hand, the person or people that say that this is the wrong way of thinking are the ones who are miserable, unhappy, unsuccessful, and do not have any peace. How could this person or people be thinking the wrong way, but are bringing themselves peace, happiness, and success? My answer is they are not thinking in the wrong direction. At least they are becoming what God wants us all to be, which as I said before happier, peaceful, and successful. So, I say keep thinking this way, because at least it is a still much better wrong way to think(figuratively speaking) if it is helping you to heal your mind and spirit. God put us all on the Earth to be rich, happy, healthy, and at peace. Obviously you are closer to God and how God wants you to think as opposed to the ones who claim to be.

[BELIEFS=EMOTIONS]

Your beliefs expresses your emotional state. This is why people talk so strongly and with conviction about their beliefs and what they believe in. Beliefs control your emotional states, whether it is beliefs about yourself, others, or anything else. Unfortunately sometimes some things that we believe in are the very things that cause mental pain, hurt, and haunt. Some beliefs limit and restrict higher and healthier ways and perspectives of thinking, being, and experiencing. There are higher and more powerful ways of states of emotion, but if your beliefs limit you from gaining a higher level of these states and experiences, you will not be able to get to those higher levels of heath, strength, and being. Beliefs are what we believe to think is true. Beliefs are formed by are perspectives and understandings, which ultimately becomes are overall perception of reality. You are taking power from yourself when you believe and have perceptions about yourself or people that causes you to maintain a distorted and unhealthy reality. Change and alter your detrimental beliefs, then this process will give you power over your emotions. Examine your emotional states, then examine your beliefs, then you will see they both have a attachment to each other. Change those unhealthy believes that bring negative emotional states and negative thinking. Ultimately everything that you believe will guide your emotional states, psychological well being, and will show up in your thoughts, focus, attitude, spirit, and energy.

[CONVERT TO OFFENSE AND DEMOTE TO DEFENSE]

Also it is helpful and healthy to develop the ability of letting your guards down. You must stop being on the defense all the time, because this will consequently destroy and negatively affect all relationships and aspects of your life. You must gain the ability of being more on the offense side of things, before putting your guards up in attack mode on defense. Acquiring pattern of automatic defense will inhibit future progression, understanding, and growth through communication among the ones you love, friends, associates and co-workers. Communication and information is the source of human existence, intelligence, and understanding. Consequently the lack of not knowing how to effectively communicate and transfer information verbally will be detrimental and will negatively affect your happiness, relationships, goals, and financial inspirations.

Maintaining an automatic defensive way of thinking will indefinitely in turn submit you to a life of misery and loneliness. It affects you personal relationships as well as work relationships. This way of thinking will present a life of miscommunication, misinterpretation, false assumptions, and false accusations. In addition this setback will present a life of chaos and confusion. Ultimately, misguided and misinformed assumptions turn into false accusations with slim to none possibilities of being even an inch of accurate and true assumptions. It is better to not assume, which will allow you to find out the truth, then to assume and find that you are inaccurately accusing someone. This breaks up happy homes and relationships, and even causes an already unhappy home and relationship to go further into misery. In judicial terms this means you are accusing someone with false misconceptions and pretenses. Furthermore you are judging someone and summoning them guilty until proven innocent. When it is suppose to be innocent until proven guilty. You will ultimately be the reason of your own isolation and despair. Sometimes I think we can be the reason of our own misery. There is a saying, Misery loves company. But, I say, "what do you do if you are the misery of your own company," (Lemon)? You will find family and friends not wanting to be in your presence, which will only present a life of misery. There are justifiable times to be defensive, but why be defensive when it's a lot easier to be offensive. If you are on the offense it will be easier to adapt to when you should be defensive. Initially adopting an offensive approach and response will present you with the following: a life of never judging anyone, better communicating skills, and levels of understanding will raise, growth, maturity, happier relationships, less stressful life, minimum frustration/ irritation, blood levels healthy, peace, being more open-minded, and less confrontational. It is too much negative energy and is time consuming always being on the defense toward everybody and everything. The time will present itself when you must defend yourself. But other than that, being open and receptive is a much healthier and powerful way of day to day relationships.

(THE BALANCE BEAM OF LIFE)

Compare your mind to a balance beam. For example, the more weight you put on one side gravitational pull will weigh that side down lower than the other side, because it is more weight on the side and heavier. Consider your mind as a balance beam of negative and positive thoughts. If you have more negative thoughts out weighing the positive thoughts that will typically become what majority consumes your mind and what develops your thought process. Which, thinking more negative than positive will only lead to a life of failure, unhappiness. However, having more positive thoughts outweighing the negative thoughts will generate a life of happiness, peace, self motivation, and financial fortune. The ultimate goal is to get you to think more positive than negative. Or to say the least to have a balance between negative thoughts and positive. So, at least you would be a little bit happier or have a balance between happiness and unhappy thoughts. For example, I'm not saying live your life in a shell of safety of monitoring every thought. Because that probably would be extremely time and energy consuming. Nor am I saying don't trust everybody and everywhere you go and stopping yourself from enjoying the excitement the world has to offer. I'm simply saying examine yourself every now and then. Also, if you see a pattern of too much negativity and bad thoughts generating, use this method of the balance beam of life to average out negativity/ positivity or better yet raise the bar of positivity over negativity. For example, math's algebra even deals with positives and negatives, which to say the least two negatives equals a positive $(-5*-2=+10)$. My point is you can get positives out of negatives and see the good within the bad even compared to life just like math. However, you cannot pull a negative out a positive (-10+9=-1) and get good higher positive results. You can't just fill your mind with all unproductive images and audio's, because it will post pone and limit your train of thought. It will stunt your mental growth of higher learning, comprehension and understanding. Furthermore, you will catch yourself aging and getting older, but your mind is far beyond and lacks nourishment and information. You must feed your mind just as you feed your mouth. Without the proper nutrition and exercise it will degenerate faster along with your physical body. We can all balance a double cheeseburger with lettuce, tomatoes, onions, and extra mayonnaise with a 7 eleven strawberry slushy, a sneaker bar, and the diet pop for even calories (laughing). But we can't take the time out to make sure our happiness is balanced by making sure we occasionally monitor our mental intake.

[MIND PURGING]

(Wash Your Brain)

I call this process of gaining more positive thoughts than negative mind purging. Follow this strategy for a day, weekend, week or however long it takes for you feel more at peace and happy. Do this little by little until you gain your happiness and peace of mind back. Do it for a day if you had a prior bad day. Do it for a weekend if you had a prior negative day. Also do it for a week if you had a prior bad week. When you watch TV or a movie watch positive, inspirational movies and funny comedy movies that make you laugh. Watch super hero movies, where the good guys win and good always win over evil. Watch movies and meet people that are ordinary, but do extraordinary things.

Also switch and change the music you listen to for a while from negative to more positive, rather it is rap, r&b, country, rock, alternative, etc. Listen to positive, encouraging, empowering music that lifts your spirits. When you go to sleep listen to the nature, stress easing melodies. When you go to sleep listen to soothing music that mentally relaxes you. This is just a way to catch your positive thoughts up to your negative thoughts. Furthermore, even better these are ways to surpass your negative discouraging thoughts and ideas. For example related to and is an extension to the passage on the balance beam of life.

TOILET MISERY

(Part 1)

Toilet misery creates definite unhappiness, bad relationships, detrimental attitudes, unproductive energy, horrible marriages, bad karma, and constant financial pot holes of debt and setbacks. Toilet misery without a doubt becomes a curse. Ultimately, Setbacks, distraction, unhappiness, and failure is the only thing to look forward to, which the byproduct inevitably will be a life of toilet misery. This is developed from off the way you are thinking. Basically, your mind is clogged up. For example, when a toilet is clogged up, what happens? It is a higher possibility everything in it, including urine and feces will eventually spill out. Let's say you took a vacation and haven't been home for two weeks. But, when you come back you was welcomed to an over flown toilet with feces and urine all over the bathroom and through the living room. Unfortunately it's not safe or sanitary to be in that house, because of mold, infection and bacteria. That house is contaminated and if not treated is destined to accumulate a disease that will spread to everyone subjected to it. Ultimately by those attaining this disease and curse will cause a shorter life span.

NEONATE POSITIVE PARENTING

(Toilet Misery)
(Part 2)

Compare a clogged toilet with feces and urine that is bound for disease to a baby that is just born into this world. This baby by the way already has the burden of being born into a negative and corrupt world. Their minds are so sensitive and when something is sensitive it's easily molded, controlled, and negatively persuaded. These babies are like a new canvas and take in everything they see and hear, because remember their minds are sensitive and weak. Typically their minds aren't strong enough to fight off negativity and corruption. This negativity is what becomes all a baby knows while growing up. It's a high possibility that these kids will grow up and become adults of negativity and corruption of crimes of murder, homicide, genocide, suicide, assault, robbery, kidnappings, etc. My point is parents must start positive parenting and clogged toilet preventative methods as soon as a child is born. Parents has to install good positive values and instill good thoughts and ideas into their kids minds as a foundation as opposed to more negative and bad thoughts and ideas. It all starts with the parents; if they do this the world will be a better place through neonate positive parenting skills.

As I said a baby is born into a negative corrupt world, so it odds are already against him or her of becoming a positive mentally healthy happy person. Also the percentages are even lower for a child to become a productive citizen who lives a healthy lifestyle and is financially well off. Furthermore, the percentages are even lower for these kids to reach 25 years old considering their corrupted negative upbringing. I don't believe this saying, "These kids now and days hear one thing in one ear and it goes out the other." When these babies are born into a negative corrupted parenting, this becomes their mindsets of being very negative and destructive. This inhibits their mental growth, enhancement, knowledge, focus, mind elevation and greatness. This mindset is adopted by them and the symptoms are low confidence, self doubt, self pity, lack of communication skills, lack of faith, lack of self empowerment, lack of self worth, poor decision making, lack of self belief, limiting themselves, no mental endurance, giving up before trying, and mentally setting themselves up for failure(defeat) before trying. They ultimately become a total failure before even trying and develop a thing called mental degeneration.

(INHERITED CLOGGAGE)

Toilet Misery
Part 3

This is an extended version of the clogged toilet. When a clogged toilet over flows it comes out in a downward motion. Which we established disease and infection is ultimately determined if not treated and sanitized. So, as I did before comparing the human mind to a clogged toilet, which the flow of a clogged toilet eventually seeps downward. In comparison to downward flow of clogged toilet is the human mind thinking in a downward negative way. For example, when we count going up, which resembles positive numbers is as follows: +5, +6, +7, +8, +9, and +10. However, when we count going down, which signifies negative numbers is as follows:-10,-9,-8,-7,-6, and-5. My point is as I said before even in numbers it's a correlation of how we should think and the impact it has on our individual lives. It is clear that thinking more negative is not the right and good way of thinking. To make a long example short regarding the clogged toilet, thinking negative is basically having a clogged toilet as a mind, which produces negative thoughts compared to feces, which ultimately develops your brain and train of thought. Then, sooner than later the effects will cause mental diseases and ultimately physical diseases.

This example of a clogged toilet mindset originates from the grandparents and the parents got it from their parents, then they pass it down to a future generation of kids and it gets worse and worse until it is sanitized. Or people develop this clogged mindset through world influence. That's exactly why I stand firm on the effectiveness of the balance beam of life insert. This all can stop if parents re train themselves first to put more positivity within their minds then negative, which this is how eventually future generations will be raised and brought up. So, in retrospect these negative clogged mindsets of mental degeneration are being inherited and passed down from parents to future generations. However, that's why I said parents have the initial influence. However, kids grow up and have the ultimate choice to make in terms of what path he or she decides to go. Unfortunately sometimes that choice was already initially decided depending upon their parental upbringing. But it is a very hard choice for some to go the good route, because all they know is bad and negativity and it becomes a more comfortable easier route in the beginning. But it is a saying that goes, "All bad things come to an end." Which the end is never good in these cases. A lot of these mental and physical diseases can be cured and even better prevented. By means of going through a process of what I call a mental rebirth and reconstructing their lives through the balance beam of life. I keep stressing if your mind is congested with more negative thoughts it will breakdown your body, soul, and spirit as well.

[A GIFT DISGUISED AS A CURSE]

"A curse lifted reveals the true power and potential of the cursed," (Lemon). Toilet misery is an insert explaining how your mind could be considered as unsanitary, which develops into a curse of toilet misery. However, a curse in disguise symbolizes that your toilet is dirty. But by it being so dirty that filth allowed you to gain a different insight then someone who never experienced such filth and such a burden. Now I'm sure you will cherish a cleaned toilet more the the average toilet owner, (laughing). A curse is not always a bad or horrible thing. "A curse can be much more of a gift than the gift itself," (Lemon). If you gain the strength to endure the pain, you will realize that curse was just a way to show you that you posses a very powerful gift. Once you see past the suffering of a curse and get through it, you can acquire the sight to understand that a curse survived will give you a gift to develop a more powerful and much deeper form of knowledge and wisdom. If you never knew what it means to suffer, how could you really know how strong you really are? Suffering and struggling is not a negative thing, because once you get through it you will gain a higher tolerance level of suffrage and will create a stronger spirit and a different connection to power. "Once the cursed realize that their curse is a gift, then this is when the cursed becomes the most powerful," (Lemon). No one will take the time out to curse anyone or purposely cause them a life time of pain if they did not fear them or ever considered them as a threat then and in the future. You must be thankful for your curse, struggle, or heavy burden. Because, if it wasn't for that, then you would have never known your true potential or how strong and powerful you really were. If it wasn't for your curse you would've never known the true power of humility and you would've never known the true power of power. Ultimately you would've never known your purpose and the true meaning of life.

(DNA OF LIFE)

There is a higher power that created us known as GOD! Also this higher power of omnipresence wants us to feel and emotionally be positive and happy. I believe the different words we use tend to have us feel a certain way too. So, words that this higher power needs us to use to make us feel alive are words of happiness, positivity, glad, cheerfulness, enjoyment, encouragement, motivation, bliss, etc. These words give us a reassurance that this is our natural way of feeling. Also these words are a way of telling us this is the way we were born to feel. Through usage of these words our mind becomes at ease, we are more driven; we are less irritated, worried and less stressful. We feel more cheerful, confident, ambitious, more esteemed and rightly guided. We feel like this is how we were created to feel and these feelings that empower us from these specific positive words are our true DNA of life. Which provides us with love, peace, and happiness? Also, we know by feeling this way keeps my mind and body healthier. It gives us the overall desire to LIVE and LOVE.

(SUN RISING POSITIVE MINDSET)

I believe the perfect example of this is our true way of mentally feeling from the one and only higher power that made us is when the sun rises and you see it rise and feel it. You feel and get an emotion that creates inspiration and that builds up which pushes you to do what you might not have done if you didn't have a spark of motivation and never give up attitude that the sun provides. Also when the sun rises our mind becomes more at ease and stimulated. This natural feeling that the sun activates gives us drive, ambition, will, energy to rise up and get out of bed and go for it! This also brings a feeling of rejuvenation and hope. Also, remember anything rises goes up and up is where the light is from, which the creator shines down on us to show us this is your true nature and up is where you want to go mentally most important. This sun rising effect gives us promise that it will be a better day. This is when people seem most positive, happy, excited, joyous, and safe. However, when the sun goes down and it becomes dark that is when if you notice it seems as though this is when some people get a little more corrupt, vicious, evil, wicked and negative. Also some people are a little less happy, sad, angry, and unsafe.

[RAGE CANNOT LIVE WITHIN THE LIGHT]

For example, in ware wolf movies the only time the wolf comes out and kills is at night when it is dark and gloomy. If you notice during the day the wolf becomes a man because, it is too much sun out, too much light out, it is too much positivity and love in the air for the wolf to be a wolf. It becomes impossible for the wolf to fill rage within his heart, because during the day of sunrise his mind, heart, and soul are filled with happiness, peace and love. However, when the sun goes down this is when he becomes posed with negativity and corruption, which becomes rage of evil acts upon humankind. This man has a burden of a curse. However there is always a way to reverse a curse. In this case the only way this curse will be lifted is if a woman he loved during the day of sunrise accumulates the courage to come within the darkness to show the wolf her light filled love as in the form of a kiss and touch that he is not truly this beast. She must show this beast who he really is during the day. Which she must reveal to him his true identity. She must win his mind, heart, and soul back through getting this beast to subside the rage and feel the love she has for him. She must have love within her eyes when she gazes through his so she can pierce his soul to bring him back to the light. Then when he sees who he really is within her eyes of love and sunshine his rage subsides. This is how the curse is reversed. In contrast to life, we must reverse our curse we put upon ourselves unless we will forever be in darkness and misery. You must love yourself and you must be you. Because being someone else doesn't fit the scope of your own DNA and make up. So, being someone else will only throw off the original fabrication of you and you will forever be lost and will never know your true identity. You must become like the sun and rise up.

DEAD MAN WALKING

(Either U Live to Die or U Die to Come Alive)

I see it as unfortunate initially we all do not have extraordinary and limitless choices, options, or decision to guide us in the direction of happiness, fortune, and peace of course only from the restricted perspective of mental imprisonment. Ultimately from a more profound and deeper standpoint, I call mental imprisonment "dead man walking!" Which I explain that we have two options, which is to live to die or die to come alive. However, you do not have an option in the beginning to choose to die to come alive, because you do not know that you are mentally imprisoned and is a dead man walking. The only way you create the second option to die to come alive is by realizing you are mentally imprisoned. I say this because of being born to live in a world of pain, hurt, terror, fear, psychological destruction, mental and emotional hurt will inevitably descend upon you insanity and mental imprisonment. "Do not live within a perception that creates a reality of deception," (Lemon). Mental imprisonment tricks you into living a complete lie. But the issue is mental imprisonment does not allow those to realize they need spiritual, mental, and psychological guidance and healing. Also some do not know about these cures and remedies that will ensure them with a much healthier life. You cannot know you need a cure or healing from something if you cannot reach a higher perspective and realization of your disease. In addition you will not know the right questions to ask or ever find a solution if you do not even realize that you are living in the very same thing that is breaking you down. People began to think and believe that this is how life is supposed to be. They think this is what comes with living. They began to think this is just life! Life is not supposed to be a feeling of death. By thinking in this way your mental and psychological issues become normal to you and you just live with it. Do not accept life as it is especially when it doesn't accept you. "Life is a gift and will not open up to anybody who takes it for granted," (Lemon). If you take life for granted, life will show you what it means to truly feel dead. I'm here to tell you this is not how life is supposed to be. When in fact there is a much healthier way to live, which will bless you with happiness, peace, and fortune. Mental imprisonment will present you with a discourse and unhealthy life that is until you disconnect from it.

(LIVE TO DIE)

Some people's minds are lost even before they begin to use it. Some will be subjected to insanity even before they get an opportunity to use their mind, as if that is a great opportunity right? The process of insanity started right from their first thought from a perspective of mental imprisonment. They don't even have a chance and I thought a chance was something that was good and allows progress and a good outcome. But in this case it's subjected to a self-destructive mental income. Their memory was already set up for them to remember tragic and traumatizing events. So their memory was never theirs in the first place. On a deeper level, the only thing that separates a person from insanity is time. So, the other option if you decide to choose it is to live to die. Meaning accepting your present and future mental state of mind that you yourself do not feel safe and happy in. Which you will live and stay in the same mind frame of mental imprisonment of misery, pain, hurt, imbalance, no knowledge of self, mental and emotional trauma, unhappiness, and no peace. It is just like you are dead, but you are still walking and breathing, inhaling, and exhaling, but what you are exhaling is misery. Ultimately eventually you have a very high possibility of going insane while accepting to dwell within mental imprisonment.

[LOST BEFORE FOUND]

Die to Come Alive!

My second way of explaining dead man walking is either you die to come alive. Which being born in and living in this world of chaos and death alone will cause mental issues and psychological malfunctions and ultimately a shut down. So I mean if you live in this world with the same mind that you initially came in with, you will be miserable and that misery possibly could lead you insane. "No one or nothing can make you miserable, unless you allow them or it to control your sanity," (Lemon).

Your other option is to either die to come alive, which means you made the choice to completely disconnect from mental imprisonment, which will give you the following: a free mind, life, new experiences, reality, power knowledge that helps you grow, prosper, and stay healthy, more opportunities, a completely new, and fresh healthy start. You are not the person you need to be while being a prisoner of mental imprisonment. You can not be the powerful human being that you are capable of being, while still a prisoner of mental imprisonment. In addition dying to come alive symbolizes going through the pain to gain the knowledge of suffering, which will sustain you and will make you stronger then you can ever imagine. Ultimately to die to come alive means to transform into a higher, profound, powerful, mentally self-sufficient, and healthier you. This is the choice you must make in order to take control of your own mind, before it becomes too late and this will cause you to go further and deeper into misery, confusion, and ultimately deeper into mental imprisonment. To die to come alive also means a break from everything that is distracting and controlling you from knowing yourself from the inside out. Which by knowing yourself will put you in the position of knowing what is best for you, knowing what your problems are, knowing the right questions to ask, knowing how to find solutions to you, and ultimately gaining back control over yourself and life through deep cleansing and rejuvenation. So in this special case it is safe to say and of course figuratively speaking that it was a good thing that you lost your mind. Because the one you had before was the reason why you was lost. "You have to choose die to come alive as opposed to living to die in order to realize that you are already dead through the way you are living,"(Lemon).

8ᵀᴴ PHASE

(Psychological Preparation:
Long-term Thinking)

When thinking ahead ultimately you will be happier as well as make more money and even becoming a millionaire or billionaire. When developing long-term thinking you will always maintain more control over your life and future. Long-term thinking allows you to develop and maintain stronger preparational and preventative skills and powers! "You should have never started if you did not prepare for the end in the beginning and those who prepare for the end from the start will always stay winning,"(Lemon). Utilizing your mind in general to look ahead and long-term presents the opportunity of making much smarter decisions and choices. So it is safe to say what we think fuels are day in terms of seconds, minutes, hours, months, and years. Which ultimately sets the tone for our life decisions, whether viewing it in short-term or long-term categories. The more you think and use your mind, the more money you will make. The people who make the most money are the thinkers of the world. "Knowledge is power, but long-term thinking prevents April showers," (Lemon). Meaning you will gain the ability to prevent thunder storms in your life and will be well prepared for rainy days. Also long-term thinking is power as well. Long-term thinking gives you the gift to become a visionary and a leader. In addition you will be able to gain much more accurate predictability skills through training of long-term thinking. You will gain the ability to prevent thunder storms in your life and will be well prepared for rainy days. Also it gives you the rare gift of wisdom. For example, these are the people who use their mind more than average or normal, scientists, great lawyers, doctors, nurses, engineers pro athletes, architects, inventors, best seller novelists, movie script writers and producers, judges, CEO's of companies, owners, presidents, etc. Long-term thinking gives people the ability to be in front of the status quo and a couple of steps ahead of the game. Typically when thinking ahead gives you more insight and better predictability skills, which will give you more accurate vision of what may come your way. It blesses you with the gift of foreshadowing. Ultimately this way of thinking will ensure you the chance to alter, cut, paste and construct the situation and your destiny before it happens. Which you can change the whole outcome of the situation leading up to and after it occurs.

You can control what happens, when it happens, how it happens and where it happens to a certain high extent. Acquiring and gaining this insight you can vividly predict all that can happen, whether negative or positive within a situation. Ultimately, we all are human, so your predictions might sometime be not as accurate, but the fact of the matter is the percentage of accuracy will be significantly higher than normal or average. Sometimes they will be just as you expected. So, if you think ahead and see more negatives then positives within a situation, what does that tell you? It tells you it is not a good choice and the odds of you going through with this decision is so low of success that by doing this you will only jeopardize your life, happiness, or financial future. If you think about all the bad things that can go wrong within a situation before making a final decision it will only bring you better and more positive results. I know thinking about the bad sounds unproductive, but sometimes it helps. Because you can minimize bad situations and circumstances by understanding how bad of a risk you would be taking. This is the positivity of negativity! It shows you what you do not need to do in order to gain better results. After thinking about all that can go wrong think long-term all that can go right, then you be the judge and make a wise decision. I know this seems like a negative tactic, but its way more positive than negative. Sometimes through thinking about and seeing the negativity that's in your path will productively sway you into the direction of positivity. This will greatly minimize problems, stress, obstacles, misery, setbacks, pain, agony, heart ache, and distractions.

Ultimately self altering your own destiny and fate toward positivity, happiness, peace, love and great wealth. You have the power of control over the events in your life, which futuristically affects your destiny and fate! You control your own destiny and fate. You have the power of your own success or failure.

I believe we determine our own destiny and fate depending upon the decisions you make presently, but if you learn to think ahead and catch your mistakes before they happen your life will be more fulfilling and long livable. Also you will not be a failure; you will become a success story. Psychological preparation is one of the keys of happiness and fortune, because you have thought ahead and now you know what it takes to achieve. Also you in a way know what to expect, what challenges you may face, and what type of people you may come in contact with. It will not be a matter of expect the unexpected, because you thought ahead to the point where the unexpected is something you already expected and was prepared for. Ultimately by psychologically thinking ahead you will have a better future analysis of what's to come by thinking before hand of what all can happen. You can review all the highs and lows, negatives and positives, ups and downs, pros and cons, the likely and unlikely and the possibilities of a situation before you make a choice. These are great ways to reroute your destiny and to make life much easier, happier, and more financially profitable and life survival skills that can and will keep you safe and alive a lot longer.

[THE SECRET]

The secret is the cure and the cure has always been a secret, which now I am now revealing through the eight phases of new life and experiences. The secret and cure for Mental Imprisonment which leads to the gift of Mental Immortality are the following: developing immunity from fear and intimidation, free your mind, develop a strong mindset/ self-intellect, develop a strong heart, develop mental awareness(character counts), Prepare and go through a mental rebirth, practicing strategies for developing definite truth, ultimate peace, happiness, and power, and develop skills of psychological preparation(long term thinking). These are the secrets to disconnecting from mental imprisonment and gaining back more control and power over your destiny, happiness, success, peace, and constructing a new life. However, you can read a book all you want, but that doesn't mean you will be guaranteed a new life and way of seeing things. You must turn into the book by practicing what's inside it, which will grantee a transformation through practicing that information. **"You must turn into the knowledge of what you are reading in order to live through it,"(Lemon).**

[MENTAL CONSISTENCY]

"If you do not practice anything, then you become nothing," (Lemon). Just as well as if you do not practice anything, you should not expect anything. You must practice, and just like anything the more you practice the better you become masters and experts at what you are learning. How can you truly believe in something that you never practice or have no discipline in? The answer is it is not possible. True believe comes with true hard to the core discipline and practice. You have to be consistent in your new mindset of positive ideas and thoughts to redevelop a more profound, healthier, elevated, enhanced mind and body. You must master the art of the Secret through practice in methods of discipline, dedication, and focus. You must go beyond and push it to the limit, which the limit is limitless, because you are the one who sets the limit of how far you will go in life. Never forget, you control your own destiny and fate. I hope everyone enjoyed this journey of developing happiness, survival skills (within the workplace as well as the streets) and financial wealth. I hope I helped, encouraged, uplifted, motivated, empowered and inspired somebody out there. After reading this far towards the end of the book I have faith that your mind is somewhat wondering and levitating with ecstasy. By now you should have mentally elevated, been set free from mental imprisonment, and have took steps to conquering your fears and intimidation's. Initially I said the sky is not the limit, but now it is just the beginning!

[CLOSING REMARKS]

Now I do believe in a scheduled destiny and fate. But, of course only if you allow that schedule to complete its course. To recourse and take control of your destiny and fate you must take the time out to gain back your focus and reach healthier levels of perspective and perception. I believe people create their own schedule of destiny and fate based upon how they think and what they think about themselves. I believe every individual person controls his or her destiny and fate to a certain huge extent by the following: how we think, what our perception is, what we focus on most time, what we give our time to focus on, what we think, the choices, decisions we make, to where we go, who we associate with, to the conversations we have, and to the friends we make. Destiny and fate is created from your own personal individual life experiences, acquaintances and reacquintances. I do not believe in people run into good luck or bad luck. I believe you run into what you make yourself. Your luck is created based upon you. You make your own luck and you either have what it takes or you don't and that's it!

I wrote this book from the perspective of someone who is already successful and happy. Whether I had money or not. In addition, I mentally took myself to happiness and financial success before physically getting there. I didn't wait until I saw it; I sped up the process and thought it, felt it, then became it. You must think and feel happiness and success before you become it! "I am my practice and if this was college I would be the student-teacher and nobody would control the curriculum but me," (Lemon).

"I AM IRRIPLACABLE, I AM UNEXPENDABLE, I AM WORTH MORE THAN MONEY, I AM WORTH MORE THAN GOLD, I AM BEYOND VALUE, I AM PRICELESS, I AM FREEDOM INFORMATION," (LEMON).